CONTENTS

FOGHORN LEGHORN REDUX

BBDB READER # 1

BBDB READER # 1

BBDB READER # 1

BBDB READER # 1

BBDB READER # 1

AFTER DENVER

FEDS ON VACATION

BEYOND

FOGHORN LEGHORN REDUX

FOGHORN LEGHORN REDUX

FOGHORN LEGHORN REDUX

FOGHORN LEGHORN REDUX

FOGHORN LEGHORN REDUX

FOGHORN LEGHORN REDUX

2019

INTERCOM

Please stay calm. Our crew is working on the

issue right now. Please stay seated with your

fingers crossed. I mean your seatbelt fastened.

I'm sorry. I don't know why I said that.

I'm not scared, and I'm running this thing, so

there's no reason why any of you should

be scared. We are all in this together.

This experience is a shared one, and

soon our bodies will be a shared one. Do

you know what I'm talking about? All of

us getting mixed in with one another,

like a party where soup is served, and we

are the soup that is being served, drinking

ourselves, everyone swallowed up at once.

YOU JUST GOT BOOMED

After S.S.

boom boom boom

you just got boomed

and I did it

I boomed you

you can call me the Boom Doctor

I have your emptied-out torso on the operating table

you are now living in a post-boom era, and

you want to assess the damages, but

seeing as you just got boomed, you no longer have the

capacity to

your memory's composure, a trapdoor on a pirate ship

the pirates say "there's a traitor in our midst" and

massacre themselves, recognition overthrown

there fly your tall tales, away from you

far immeasurably away, a star behind a star behind a star

you want to put your finger on the source of the

boom (me)

but your finger, split myriad from the tip, a limp squid

hanging in the dark water

I'm sorry, did that hurt?

I didn't mean to hurt you, but

let's rewind the tape for old time's sake:

doom doom doom

I just got doomed

and you did it

you doomed me

take a look at those wondrous doom-magnets in action

ripping your wisdom teeth out while you try to make fun

of the dentist through your sleep

your hypnotic calculator reciting the inanities of the sun

your language crawling through the bog, coated in cattails

and mud

lost in the about-ness of it, submerged in the training

room ice bath

your air bubbles floating up and popping at the surface

like petty apologies

while I watch with absurd patience your death-defying

approximation:

the invisible man, dressed in bandages that you unravel

and wind yourself into

betraying me with your newness

you give me a bum (w)rap, make me look like a mistake

don't worry, shatter-eyes, your time will come

has come, is come

you can call me the Welcome Mat

you can call this the door

the wall between us goes boom, and

our heart fills the house

do you remember feeling vulnerable

when you thought you saw me coming, the

ancient, blurred look on my face?

I thought I saw a hollow look on yours

GAINING BACK THE UPPER HAND

I'm not a criminal. I'm a prison.

I incubate transgression. Duck duck goose.

More like duck duck duck, ad infinitum.

I stay ducking geese—supremely lucky.

Dry shit is just ash. We burn our food from

the inside out. Bile weasels into sky.

I'm saying everything old. A cellar

janitor, hang a mirror facedown from

the roof and I'll smear heaven with sewage.

Outer space has abandonment issues.

The latest plague received a damning score

on an aptitude test. What's news to God?

Let's catch the apocalypse with its pants

down, make it suck on our hot soft plastic.

AN EXCITING NIGHT
(I'M AFRAID IT MADE ME WANT TO DO MORE)

When my mom called and said her dad's health was

failing fast, that we'd be leaving early

the next morning to drive 1200 miles

to her hometown in Wisconsin, I was

high on coke at a friend's birthday party.

I wanted to go back home right then, but

I was so high. I told a room full of

people, some of whom I didn't know, that

my grandfather was dying. I put on

a song and the person whose birthday it

was said, "This is too sad," and turned it off.

Did I snort coke after I found out, though?

I don't think I did, but can't say for sure.

While we were gone, a bunch of her plants died.

69 REMAKES (PART 1/3)

Remake of *The Matrix* that's security cam footage of me drunkenly breaking into a Best Buy and passing out with a VR headset on.

Remake of *Memento* where I'm stoned in a room trying to remember what I was talking about.

Remake of *Batman* where I walk around at night in a cheap mask hitting cops in their ribs and shins with a bat while shrieking dementedly.

Remake of *Life of Pi* where I fall off the raft and drown in the first 5 minutes and the rest of the movie is a 2-hour shot of the ocean.

Remake of *Bloodsport* where I spend an hour and a half trying to do the splits and rip open my taint and bleed out on a gymnastics mat.

Remake of *Say Anything* where I show up uninvited at my father's funeral holding a boombox over my head playing "Hippa to da Hoppa" by Ol' Dirty Bastard.

Remake of *Man on Fire* where I return to my old high school, self-immolate with kerosene, and, bellowing madly, tackle my football coach.

Remake of *Home Alone* where I break into my dad's house, hide in his bed with a knife, and, when he finds me, calmly say, "tuck me in, motherfucker."

Remake of *Top Gun* where the gun is at the bottom.

Remake of *Speed* where I give out weed and brandy on a Megabus, incite a riot, and drive it off an overpass into a sports stadium during a game.

Remake of *The Running Man* where I intercept my dad during his morning jog and chase him down the street with a knife.

Remake of *The Deer Hunter* where I, wearing a large deer hide, hold my dad hostage and force him to play Russian roulette with me.

Remake of *Die Hard* where I am, until I meet death's all-forgiving embrace, haunted by the undying memory of the time I met Bruce Willis.

Remake of *Homeward Bound* where the pets eat the family when they get back because they turned feral and are starving to death.

Remake of *The Mighty Ducks* about strong ducks.

Remake of *Air Bud* where, in the last seconds of the final game, the CIA assassinates the dog because it's actually a Russian spy.

Remake of *Commando* where I attend a gun show wearing nothing but a camouflage jockstrap and buy every gun there to "assassinate my ass."

Remake of *Little Miss Sunshine* where I skip around a Whole Foods wearing nothing but a diaper drooling and playing a ukulele and toy xylophone.

Remake of *The Lion King* called *The Truthin' King* about a king who doesn't lie.

Remake of *Gone with the Wind* where I leave with the wind.

Remake of *3 Ninjas* where I accost three boys on a sidewalk and demand they karate chop me to death.

Remake of *3 Ninjas Kick Back* where I, wearing casts and wrapped in bandages, accost three boys on a sidewalk and demand they kick me to death.

Remake of *3 Ninjas Knuckle Up* where I am visited in the hospital by three boys and, barely able to speak, I say, "finish it, you pussies."

LENGTHENING THE STORM OR HOW TO BE BELIEVABLY FRAGILE

Fit as many fingers as you can

inside the gaping hole of my

rhetoric. I mean it—really stretch out that assumptive

void. It won't hurt me, or I won't act

hurt, unless you expect me to,

in which case I'll compete

for the affection of algorithms

against my peers, who climb

pine trees, which makes this swaying

and yowling in the wind in the name

of ghosts I'm doing a little explicable,

and when I say a little, I mean

a Chicken Little. I say The sky is falling,

but mean I'm falling through the sky like rain.

I'm doing this on purpose says

the textile factory collapse. I didn't mean

to hurt you says the hippo, child in jaw—

contorted pomegranate. They tell

the truth, which is why it makes

little sense to anybody other than chickens

with their heads cut off, doing what they know best.

And here we are

on the other side of the electric fence,

barbed snotty weeds

sprouting from the cracked ground,

people in passing cars

not thinking to notice us, and even if they did,

we wouldn't be enough for them to pull over

and stare—advancing along the highway,

its inbuilt purpose, hearing static chew

pop songs on the radio

like lumps of gum with dirt in them, gazing through

frames grayed by runny splays

of what were once shiny flying bugs.

Falling through the sky, by grace

I grabbed to a tiny rickety wing

of a single engine Cessna

that, after bending loud tight loops

above a dispassionate reptilian crowd, landed

on a desolate bow of road in the waste. But the sky—

the sky keeps falling through me

without landing, like a shadow that can't

find the floor. Maybe, if you fit a dry hand

inside me, you can cease this hysteria, or at least

I won't be so wet and swift. Maybe, if you fit

yourself inside me, I'll run out of air

to talk with, and I'll rest for the first time

since you showed at the door

I don't live behind anymore. You'll turn around

and get in your car, and I'll be in the

passenger seat, unconscious and under

your care, like I've been this entire time—just faking

wakefulness. What we have is special. To the rest

of the world (where soon we'll be) we look

like mutes, like rain before it hits, before it's no longer

rain.

GAY RODNEY DANGERFIELD

I tell ya it's hard going to the movies when you're gay, ya know? I took my straight 14-year-old nephew, whose favorite comedian is Amy Schumer, to see her new movie, I Feel Pretty. I, on the other hand, being gay, had to see I Feel Pretty Gay.

I tell ya it's hard going grocery shopping when you're gay, ya know? The other day I went to Trader Joe's and accidentally ended up penetrating two pistachio mochis I'd squeezed together and forgot weren't butt cheeks.

I tell ya I get no respect as a deeply repressed gay man, ya know? Why, just the other day I was making love to the superimposed, mentally projected image of my old man top of my wife's face and I said, "Say 'good job' when I cum." S/he told me I should only take pride in my work!

I tell ya it's hard getting a driver's license when you're gay, ya know? Just the other day I was getting mine renewed and the DMV clerk asked if I was an organ donor. "It's not the kind of donation where you get to keep it after you pull it out of his asshole," he added.

I tell ya I get no respect as a severely closeted gay man, ya know? Just the other day I was driving my yellow Nissan Xterra to buy a cup of gorilla taint flavored fro-yo. This guy in a way less cool car than mine cut me off. Needless to say I lost my appetite and had sex with him.

I tell ya it's hard having parents when you're gay, ya know? When I came out to my mom, she had to deal with both the disappointment of me never having children in a heterosexual marriage, and even worse, the crushing let down of knowing I'd never have sex with her again.

I tell ya it's hard being a hopelessly closeted gay man married to a woman with three children, ya know? I want to tell them the truth, but if I did, it would tear my family apart, not to mention my asshole.

I tell ya it's hard getting a car wash when you're a tyrannized queer, ya know? It took everything in me to refuse the "clear coat" I wanted but couldn't afford.

I tell ya it's hard eating pizza when you're gay, ya know? Why, if my memory serves me well, it was just the other night that I ordered a thin crust sausage and green bell pepper pizza. I had the worst acid reflux that night. It's hard enough burning at one end!

I tell ya it's hard watching Will & Grace when you're gay, ya know? It's almost like the characters' homosexuality being consistently used for punchlines your family laughs at in their "acceptance" of you makes you feel somehow even more ashamed and less like an individual.

HOLOGRAM BABY

Baby I'm a disposable camera.

Baby you stop me dead in my tracks, burn a hole in my brain.

Baby I'm your biggest fan, I'm wearing your t-shirt, can't you read the pop-calligraphy?—can't you recognize your own handwriting?

Baby I've got filing cabinets full of dreams you wrote, my office is dripping with dream-juice, my hands are holding fresh dollar bills, ready to spend on you.

Baby you make it all seem worthwhile, you get me out of

bed in the morning, you make the coffee taste hopeful, you make me leave the house with confidence and go to the office where I fill cabinets with dreams of you.

Baby take these handcuffs off of me, now put them back on.

Baby your picture exposes the end of what I desire, which is the beginning of what I desire, a road paved in dreams.

Baby the cacti are singing me road directions.

Baby I'm confused, the world is changing—quick, tell me something I can trust for even a second because I can't come up with anything good.

Baby stop hiding in the utility closet.

Baby stop looking like an angel.

Baby don't open your mouth, don't ruin the suspense

worked so hard to sustain.

Baby my hair is standing on end, my nerves scrambling to catch up with you, playing possum in the moonlight.

Baby the wise know their foolishness well.

Baby you were cast in bronze, racing headlong toward me through a hot glass tunnel.

Baby the glass is cracking, you're humming in my ears like a flute.

Baby thinking of you like this is a holy tradition at this point.

Baby I see you across the room at the party, I can't hear you, but from the look on your face I can tell what you're talking about—you're talking about finding the disease in me.

Baby the world is hungry and so are we, but we're harm-
less enough you and I—tadpoles in a puddle of tears.

Baby you may be my baby but I feel just like a child when
it comes to you, I'm trying to stay warm in the nest you
built.

Baby puke inside my mouth, tell me something I can strap
my heart to with a horse-hide belt.

Baby fire is quiet and painless and ice is a punishing
screech in the wild.

Baby our bodies are being destroyed and I can't turn my
eyes away from you.

Baby I'm sorry for being dramatic but the world, inex-
plicable and cancerous, moves like an insect across the
ceiling.

Baby was that you on the side of a building, riding a golden wagon in the sunset?

Baby I hope I'm right on target, hope I'm reaching you clear.

Baby are you tuned in?—is this making any sense?

Baby our kingdom has epilepsy, we live in a sensitive fortress, we might have to smuggle ourselves out in disguise to survive.

Baby you're just over this hill, just around this corner, just through this door, I can see your shadow hinting safety from where I stand, I'll follow the necessary logical steps.

Baby we're ruthless when we talk to each other, do we really believe it's fun to drag this cruel contest out?

Baby I have to go to the bathroom, if you don't have an excuse to shut your eyes I'd be glad to give you one if it'll help, because baby, I'm here to help.

Baby we are commas in each other's breaths, hitches in each other's steps.

Baby we only want to feel what we heard feels good.

Baby let's put on the rubber gloves and go on a rampage, we'll have the town talking for weeks.

Baby gossip flings off of us effortlessly: all we do is tell ourselves stories, we're a force to be reckoned with.

Baby what are we doing now?—let's find another problem we can't solve.

Baby you remind me I'm not yet finished with the task at hand, your tent glowing on the mountainside, I can smell the smoke from the meadow below.

Baby I'll be there soon, don't fall asleep yet, it's cold, I'll make my way up the mountain in the dark.

Baby I have no way of knowing what I've done, I'm walking to you without a person to count on.

98 DOLLARS

While working

Smoking a cigarette outside the bar

That I bummed from my boss Tom

A gay couple I served earlier

It is a gay bar after all

Comes walking down the sidewalk

Side by side, I don't know

Where they went

But they are back now

Smiling at me sitting in

An orange plastic chair

In light rain, two other

Presumably straight guys

Come walking the other way

As they pass one of the gay guys
Says something flirtatious
To the straight guys
His boyfriend turns to me and says
"Can you see why I love him?"

I say no I can't see why
And don't see how anyone
Other than he can see why
He loves him

He says "ah, you've
Outsmarted me"
I didn't say this but
I didn't outsmart him
I didn't out anything him

After closing walking home
Raining harder now

I see

A man asleep under a storefront awning

His head on his shoes

A woman asleep under a church arch

Her belongings around her body

Outside a dive close by my house

Torn up playing cards

From an abandoned three-card Monte game

I don't know why someone

Loves someone

I don't know why

The jackal fails

I don't see how I

Can ever fall asleep

Just like that

I made 98 dollars in tips tonight

My housemate let me in through the kitchen

In the basement because I forgot to

Bring my keys when I left

I was lucky he was still up

DEVIL BOTTOMLESS

I'm being discovered by the historians a thousand years from now and they're not impressed.

I'm digging a hole, squandering every last piece of darkness.

I'm in bed with the phone held close while the Devil dreams to me on the other end of the line, swings his pocket-watch in front of my face in flashes, pours gunpowder in my ears with a funnel, which is his mouth, and camouflages himself into tired pictures of the earth.

I'm mesmerized and seized by the trembling fist of his visions.

I don't remember him, but I remember what he told me, and now I say it like he said it, like a lie being emptied of form.

A lie is something clever enough to allow.

To allow a lie is to sneak the Truth away from yourself for as long as you can bear the work.

It's never again, forever.

Always like this, a rotten baby.

I'm instant gone excited in the grave.

It doesn't work.

I've dissected the world as small as I can and have wrapped everything in bacon.

Space is fat with the prospect of purpose and grossly in-

incomplete.

I'm taking deep breaths of stones.

I'm looking through a man who's looking at a man try-
ing to say something about himself, where he stands, what
accounts for what, how he got this grotesque, who it was
that pinned him down in the night and forced on him a
story to live by, something to help him move more easily,
a physical clue, instructions and explanations that suggest
who he is and what makes the inside cough on the outside,
that there's a difference, that there's a secret to know, that
the organs are doors that transport the miraculous and
commonplace.

When he tries to make things simple, they become com-
plicated, when he tries to make anything into anything, it
becomes nothing at the same time.

The harder he looks at it, the harder it looks to him.

I'm discovering my cadaver a thousand years from now and it looks nothing like me.

I look nothing like me.

My eyes look like an incoming snowstorm.

My look looks like a man in a coma whose flesh is on fire and he's stinking up the whole room and all is lost, and lost begins again and so do I.

Magician the tailor measuring dreams dramatic.

Ark of wound massive hemorrhaging memory taking drunken soldiers hostage, bathing in terror, laughing in green and red valleys and cheeks.

Bone blinks.

Action negatives.

Devil face.

Scream forever.

Remember his song.

Forget what it sounds like.

Last thing you hear is wind blowing clear through the vastest canyon.

Last thing you feel is heat.

Last thing you think is chains.

Last thing you are is life.

69 REMAKES (PART 2/3)

Remake of 3 Ninjas: High Noon at Mega Mountain where Hulk Hogan and I are a gay married couple raising three wonderful boys.

Remake of Baby's Day Out where I crawl across a metro area licking people's calves.

Remake of Dances with Wolves where I lead a pack of wolves wearing leather jackets into a dance club and we do a really cool dance routine.

Remake of Child's Play about an elementary school-aged playwright.

Remake of Honey, I Shrunk the Kids where I shrink myself and shoot myself out of a BB gun back into my mother's uterus.

Remake of Saturday Night Fever where I sit alone in a basement in a kiddie pool filled with ice water.

Remake of Adventures in Babysitting where my babysitter gives me a blowjob.

Remake of Predator where my babysitter gets charged with sexual assault after giving me a blowjob.

Remake of It where I dress up like a clown and crawl down a sewer drain to look for my childhood.

Remake of Good Will Hunting where I walk into a bar and double jump kick both Ben Affleck and Matt Damon in their chests with steel-toe boots.

Remake of Big Trouble in Little China where my asshole,

affectionately nicknamed "Little China," gets gaped by a guy named "Skirt Rustle."

Remake of Every Which Way But Loose where I get revenge on "Skirt Rustle" by crushing his hand bones in the grip of my extremely tight asshole.

Remake of Mannequin where I con my way into the conceptual art world by driving a remote control motorcycle with a mannequin on it through MoMA.

Remake of Mission: Impossible where I retrieve a free slice of pizza from a visiting writer reception without interacting with anyone.

Remake of Silver Linings Playbook where I enter a break-dancing competition and, attempting a shoulder roll, break my neck.

Remake of The Wolf of Wall Street where a wolf who can smell how rich people are stalks Wall Street biting throats in descending order.

Sequel to Big called Small where I get turned into a pre-pubescent with the same mind as I have now and kill my-self.

Remake of Finding Forrester where Bob Dylan stabs a basketball with a switchblade and, chain-smoking, beats Haruki Murakami in a marathon.

Remake of Jaws that's a "character study" of Jaws from the James Bond movies where he's suffering from clinical depression.

Remake of Can't Hardly Wait called Can't Softly Wait where a waiter goes to boot camp to learn how to be a tough waiter.

Remake of Jumanji where I squat in a mansion for a year and master a Robin Williams impression, then lead a stampede thru the SF Bay Area.

Remake of Flight of the Navigator where I break into a Tesla, hide, and, when discovered by the owner(s), say, "take me home with you."

Remake of Billy Elliot about a boy who, growing up in a culture where all boys are expected to become ballet dancers, wants to be a professional boxer.

150 DOLLARS

Sunday at the bar it's dead I'm
the only person there until an
old fat guy comes in

sits down and orders a Coke
says he's from Chicago just
passing through

seeing if he can find college
guys to sell him their
underwear

I say "oh yeah? how much do
you pay for them?"

he says "50 dollars usually

and 100 dollars

if they piss or come on them"

it's dead at the bar so I say

"sure but I'm not in college

and I'm not wearing underwear

I'm wearing a jockstrap"

he says "that's okay could you piss

on it a little?"

I say "I don't have to piss

but give me 5 minutes"

I go into the back area of the bar

by the walk-in cooler

and remove my boots then jeans

and jockstrap then put back on my

jeans then boots and walk over to

the sink where there is a bottle of

Trader Joe's hand lotion

I press down on the pump squirting

a quarter-sized amount of lotion

into the palm of my hand

I go to the women's bathroom

because it has a lock

one of those rudimentary locks

where a hook attached to the door

goes in a hoop attached to the frame

I masturbate to my reserve

of go-to images and situations

and am able to come quite fast

which surprises me

I forgot I could come so fast

because when masturbating for pleasure

I tend to prolong and savor it

when in this case I am providing a service
I feel proud that I have that kind of control
to come under pressure and expectation

and to deliver a product promptly
I step out of the bathroom smiling
and hand the old fat guy the jockstrap

"here you go"
he lifts the jockstrap
presses it into his face and inhales deeply

through his nose and exhales
through his mouth saying "oh yeah
could you show me your dick?"

I say "I really can't at the bar I'm working"
he says "can I feel your dick through your jeans?
I'll give you 50 more dollars"

I say "okay sure" and for a minute

he feels my dick through my jeans

with his hand squeezing it

while holding the underwear to his face

I get anxious and bored and say "okay

I have to get back to work"

he hands me 150 dollars and says "thank you"

I say "sure"

after a while he finishes his Coke and leaves

later about 30 minutes until the end of my shift

the old fat guy walks back in

sits down and orders a Coke

I prepare the bar

for the next person to work

I clock out and as I'm leaving say

"bye" to the old fat guy

and he says quietly

"are you interested

in earning any more money?"

I say "no"

he says nervously as if to avert

making a scene "okay no problem

no problem"

CRAB CAKE

Do not discuss the raking of our fin-
gers through our hair to lubricate our scalps
with oil from pores that seep in gaps of anx-
ious thoughts bewildered by a certitude
we ideate as having been detached
from us, but listen here, if you can find
that home from which you left, that birth, that for-
gone memory itself, that sheath of na-
da that ejected you in plasmic ex-
position when you sensed without homun-
cular ablation, rot, and did not know
what was not known and bore no images.
Don't move, don't moan, don't look for what you are
already. Light is death the fastest way.

DISPERSING ANXIETY

dispersing anxiety by imagining ripping off your own nipples and shoving them in your ears like ear plugs after hearing a person talk in that vacuous "using big words to sound smart but not talking about anything" way for over a minute

cartoonishly spraying them in the face with your nipple blood, collapsing to the ground with two dark red holes in your chest, smiling, hearing nothing but the reserve of blood leave your head, the exiting warmth

you die, then come back as that person, talking, surrounded by giant open human mouths moving up and down as that person, you stop talking, and the mouths frown

"good," you say

as that person, you jump really hard toward a vacant
baby stroller and transform midair into a baby before
you land

as that baby, you shit yourself and fall asleep
you wake up pushing the stroller off a parking garage and
into an alleyway dumpster four stories below

"goodnight," you say, "now you truly have nothing
to prove"

you jump off the parking garage and, as you fall, you see
the baby's sleeping open mouth; you shrink to the size of
a coin and fall into it

you wake up choking and cough a quarter into my palm

I'm rich now, so I don't need to talk

CHAT COMPRESSION

Genuflect down the Eustachian tube of

your own neuroatypicality.

Everyone's lives as inside one-liners.

Nothing is funny. I laugh all the time.

The currency is bad science fiction.

Dead mammal gazes only aspiring to

zombiehood. Crypts packed with stuffed animals

all lonely for me. Blow a stale kiss to

the redemption paradigm, enter the

Sad Real Now, where your own mother sees the

waste of flesh you are. Orgasms of deep

identification. Haunted shitmode.

The big diapers of understanding, in

the cheap air conditioning they're preserved.

BOYS

It could, I suppose, in theory, be plau-
sible, but, despite the desirabil-
ity of my milkshake, would I really
want all the boys in the yard? The wild ho-
moeroticism of everyday
life. The NFL seems like the propa-
ganda wing of the US militar-
y. American football games are com-
mercials for corporate proxy wars. The
way cocaine makes straight guys give candid, un-
solicited, detailed accounts of their
relationships with their dads. Saying, "I
can become anything," before veering
into oncoming traffic. "Veiled," not "wild."

MRS. DOUBTFIRE 2

Mrs. Doubtfire 2, forever wandering the corridors of would-be genius.

Epiphanies pulled from us just before the moment of awakening.

Mrs. Doubtfire 2, in which Sally Field peels back the flesh of her own visage, only to reveal the face of Mrs. Doubtfire beneath.

In which Mrs. Doubtfire hitches a ride on an errant drone, face flapping, shouting "Haloooo" at the top of her voice—pan out to the silent desert.

In which Mrs. Doubtfire immolates a group of voice-over actors with a flamethrower. "My first day as a woman and I'm already getting hot flashes."

In which Mrs. Doubtfire sodomizes Pierce Brosnan in a vicious pantomime of the Heimlich maneuver as Harvey Fierstein rubs his eyes with cayenne.

In which the cobra hood of Harvey Fierstein unfurls. In which Harvey Fierstein spits venom.

I think we'll have to go to the next level: latex.

In which Brosnan's spent viscera leaks out as Mrs. Doubtfire walks off. "I don't work with the males, 'cause I used to be one."

In which Sally Field plays *Jumanji* with Bonnie Hunt. In which Sally Field is hit by a Guinness truck. It was the drink that killed her. It was a run-by fruiting. It was David Alan Grier in the parlor with the candlestick.

Mr. Hillard, do you consider yourself humorous?

In which the little girl from *Matilda*'s mouth fills with blood.

In which the little girl from *Matilda* appears in the dark at your bedside at 3am, whispering: sink the sub hide the weasel park the porpoise a bit of the old humpty dumpty little jack horny the horizontal mambo, hmm? The bone dancer Rumpleforeskin baloney bop a bit of the old cunning linguistics.

I am Job.

Do you speak English?

I am Job.

In which Mrs. Doubtfire eats a salad made from the toes of babies and Mercedes hood ornaments while singing "Dude Looks Like A Lady." In which Steven Tyler peels back the flesh of his own visage to reveal Steven Tyler as Mrs. Doubtfire in *Jumanji*.

In which the faces of women are collected in jars. I'm ready for my close-up, Mr. Demille.

In which Matthew Lawrence melts like a sno-cone in Phoenix as the theme song from Blossom plays on a loop. Nanu Nanu.

In which Mrs. Doubtfire peels back the flesh of her own visage only to reveal the face of Sally Field as Bonnie Hunt in *Jumanji*.

In which Mrs. Doubtfire is only certain about flames.

In which I must look like a yeti in this get-up.

In which Mr. Sprinkles the mailman knocks on the door and Mrs. Doubtfire answers. "Oh, a big knock on the door! Who could it be and do we have enough time?"

"Mr. Sprinkles, boys and girls! Hello Mr. Sprinkles!"

In which Mr. Sprinkles the mailman peels back the flesh of his own visage only to reveal a glass face containing a diorama of Mrs. Doubtfire opening the door to find Mr. Sprinkles, as marionette, peeling back the flesh of his own visage only to reveal Mrs. Doubtfire.

In which Mrs. Doubtfire, deep sea in a bathyscaphe, telepathically encounters a narwhal. Kill me, it entreats her. I have a horn which contains the ache of men's bile, the accumulation of the moment an arm is poised to hurl a harpoon. The moment of baleen. The moment of Mrs. Doubtfire peeling back the flesh of her own visage only to reveal a smoldering pile of auks. I am somehow the unicorn of the sea. How is that possible? "Oh no dear, I think they've outlawed whaling."

In which Mrs. Doubtfire follows the Ho Chi Minh Trail, follows the Ho Chi Minh Trail.

In which the eyes of children in a room tear up simulta-
neously, dioramas of the ocean. An old woman is walking
from their house for the last time. She knows this.

All my love to you, poppet, you're going to be alright.
Bye-bye.

SUPER BOWL IN REVERSE

I'm going to Disneyland—one, two, three.

The Magic Kingdom needs Prince Violent

whose helmet hosts plunderous alphabets,

trades the chariots in for fighter jets.

Coliseum box seats hate to see Moors

joyous, prefer respectability,

would rather them not celebrate, have class,

be grateful, march solemn to locker rooms,

give back to their communities, because

owners won't—Space Mountain morality,

stadium lights military grade, "We

have you surrounded. Leave with your hands down."

Remember, we made you—a father-like

nutritional supplement. You owe us.

GOLDEN TRIANGLE, SETX

After J.R.

platinum feathers gleam beneath the mire;

refinery smog warps hunter orange;

hydrocracker unbraids cotton wreckage,

splits wax into clouds, beards the firmament;

birds dance, blood wings; cancer masks, silver lungs;

pus eyes, tallow systems; nauseous hatred,

ringing out; toxic shapes, sad histories;

family, friends, lovers; distorted, gone;

daddies cook venison gumbo in huts;

assault rifles bordering Walden Swamp;

gasoline plumes, iridescent Copa;

bone flocks, mist dome, emerges Realnesstree;

we wear this world that wears on us so that

it passes over us, misses itself

WALKING THROUGH

we were staying at your friend's place

a small apartment up two long stairways

while he was gone

we had a flight that evening

we had recently come back from walking around

you asked me if I wanted to smoke

I said yes

you told me to make sure the door wasn't locked

or to not shut the door behind me if it was

you walked out the door, down the hall

and out another door to the fire escape

I followed you, shutting the door behind me

I joined you on the highest platform of the fire escape

from where we could look down into the gutters

you said you didn't lock the door, did you?

I went to the door and wasn't able to turn the locked knob

I looked back at you

you thought I was joking

or were hoping I was

but could tell I wasn't

I put my hands in my hair, cursed and apologized

I said I thought it wasn't locked

I locked the knob out of habit when I came in and forgot

what are we going to do?

we left our wallets inside, your phone inside

my phone was in my pocket, but it was about to die

you tried to finesse the door open

said fuck it and kicked the door

the sound of wood splitting

we got in

now the door was broken

the area around the latch was cracked, splintered, bulging

the deadbolt was fine

I unscrewed the strike plate from the side of the door

different pieces leapt out

and tinkled onto the floor

we looked up videos to figure out how to repair it

then gave up after about an hour and a half

of trying to hold the unfamiliar metal pieces and springs

in place

while shoving them in the hole

we had to be at the airport in a few hours

I called a locksmith

he showed up and told us the latch was shot

bent from kicking in the door

repair wasn't possible, only replacement

he left to get a new latch

while you left to get us lunch

while I stayed and waited for the locksmith

you got back and we ate on the front steps

the locksmith came back

installed a new latch in the brittle, damaged hole

we left, bought glue, came back

I squeezed the door as it dried

we had sex in the bathroom

shared a cigarette looking

across the balmy city, tops of other houses

the sky turning soft around bridge lights

we made the airport without issue

had what we told ourselves were our last cigarettes

outside the terminal next to flight attendants

we fixed the door, or got it fixed together

your friend won't find out

until—unless—you tell him (you should)

when you said it felt like we were doomed from the start

I thought that was cheap

what doesn't look doomed, walking through its ruins?

I got a message from the future today

it told me not to bother

but I wasn't here to hear it

69 REMAKES (PART 3/3)

Remake of *Dog Day Afternoon* where I rob a bank and adopt 500 dogs who I train to "crowd surf" me everywhere on their backs in a roving horde.

Remake of *Escape from New York* where I live my entire life without ever traveling to New York.

Remake of *Heavyweights* where a group of healthy children get sent by their parents to a summer camp designed to make them morbidly obese.

Remake of *Daddy Day Care* where all the kids die because the dads don't know what they're doing/aren't really dads/just named the daycare that.

Remake of *The Saint* where Val Kilmer gets locked in a padded room in a straitjacket, yet he continues to perform various disguises, voices.

Remake of *The Indian in the Cupboard* called *The Dad in the Cabinet* where I find a tiny version of my dad in my kitchen cabinet and eat him.

Remake of *Tremors* where I attempt to wean myself off an alcohol habit without having a seizure/dying from withdrawals.

Remake of *Marley & Me* called *Charlie & Me* where I marry Charles Manson, break him out of prison, and we move to Alaska to train sled dogs.

Remake of *American Beauty* where the American public admits to themselves that they adored Kevin Spacey precisely because he's a creepy pedo twink chaser.

Remake of *They Live* where the guy puts on the special

sunglasses but it just shows him the wounded, spoiled child at the core of a bunch of people.

2nd Remake of *Die Hard* where I spend Christmas Eve barefoot in an abandoned building drinking champagne and listening to Sade with Reginald VelJohnson.

Remake of *Mr. Smith Goes to Washington* where I try to pass a law that makes cutting a loaf of bread unevenly punishable by death.

Remake of *Psycho* where I dress up like my mother (I don't kill anyone, I just flawlessly dress up like my mother and lead, dressing up like my mother in a manner that aspires to exact replication aside, a plain life).

Remake of *Father of the Bride* called *Father of the Side* where the father of an engaged man's mistress eats beans and franks alone in a small apartment.

Remake of *Lord of the Rings* where I spend the remainder

of my days mastering the art of ring juggling, bringing direct joy to thousands of children across the globe, never to read Tolkien's trilogy.

Remake of *What Women Want* called *What Asses Want* where I gain the ability to telepathically eavesdrop on the surprisingly sentient and discursive interior monologues of various asses and learn, through the false security of their private candor, they're not too pleased with me!

Remake of *The Graduate* where, whether I graduate or not, I'll be 55K in debt and be qualified for the same jobs as I was before I earned (or didn't) a BA in writing and literature.

Remake of *George of the Jungle* where, walking through a rainforest, I encounter George Saunders crouched on the ground wearing a safari hat (turns out he's tripping balls and communicating with insects, snakes, lemurs, etc.)

Remake of *Brokeback Mountain* where I deeply inhale the

faint but unmistakable scent of my perished lover through the fabric of his left-behind denim jacket, and, jumping off a mountain in a flying wingsuit to spread his ashes, I break my back.

Remake of *There's Something About Mary* I unwittingly participated in when this guy I dated wore my cum in his beard to the bar after servicing me.

Remake of *Altered States* where I lock myself in a room and force myself to watch 10 Steven Seagal movies in a row taking 2 hits of LSD/2 hours.

Remake of *True Lies* where I get in the wet concretefilled hole with the nuclear warhead draped in the USA flag and give a Terminator 2: Judgement Day style thumbs-up.

Remake of Click where I point the magic remote control at earth and press "off."

YOUR FIRST REAL BOYFRIEND

I'm going to be your first real boyfriend

I'm going to show you the meaning of suffering

I'm going to show you how to love another man

How to shower him with love and urine

I'm going to be your first real love

I'm going to break your shell by breaking my shell on your shell

I'm going to chisel away at that monster

I'm going to make rage funny

Your boyfriend will frown

I'm going to attack you with patience and imagination

For every thing I say, there are ten things I don't say

I'm going to torture you with the knowledge that I think
you're worthy of a robust love

For every thing I write, there are hidden cities of animals
living in complex, yet unaware systems of bunkers under
domestic objects, mating and killing

I'm going to show you the meaning of romance

I don't know the meaning of romance

That is romance

Your boyfriend will write to you in a conversational tone
he doesn't think of as poetry

I'm going to be your first real engagement with poetry

I'm going to show you how to make a world that isn't a
Walt Disney World, or a World of Warcraft

I'm going to show you how to let loose and be fun and
social

I'm not going to do that

Your boyfriend will neither lie nor cheat

Your first real boyfriend

I'm going to be your father and your son at the same
time

AWARD SPEECH

There are going to be people
along the way who will try to
inoculate you with patronizing
counsel. You should feign
gratitude, thank them for their
guidance, then run away, because
they are tormented and need you
as an object of their help in order
to locate power in their shrunken
sense of might. They will throw
darts in the dark at a thing called
"you." Honey, they are talking
about themselves. First, I would
like to thank God for

empowering me to not fall prey
to the agendas of these phony
motherfuckers. Speculation will
be made concerning your
motivation. You don't have to
bare wilderness to any hungry
strategy. Just say, "You'll have
to feel this way on your own."
You'll be dead by the time your
letter arrives. Like a vial of
poison with your name on it, the
conceit of any onlooker will be
slipped in a drink your mouth
will be too cremated to address.
This is so unexpected. I'm
rambling; I'm speechless. I'm
going viral as I gyrate the gospel.
As with the music at your
funeral, you will be escorted
offstage by the limits of
sentimentality. You will be

saying something different, but the village will be busy burning itself down. For those I've forgotten to mention, you know who you are, and I thank you for your guidance. Let the spectral orgy now obscure the acid issuing from my muscles drunk on hell. I'm honored and humbled to even be included in the category of Best Liar among these amazing, talented liars. This is for you. My children are my heroes, obviously, but you all are my war heroes, you just don't know it yet. See if you can see my eyes through the smoke. There's so much more work to be done, but we've come a long way from feeling right in the world.

METAL SPIKES

People who aren't you hold tenderizing
hammers always, so it is hard to be
juicy, clueless around them, constantly
swinging. Hello my name is flank steak, nice
to become a nerve grid under your hand.
What's missing from before and after ads
is the displaced mass. Where did it all go?
Temptation explains "away" or "down the
drain." If wishes were computers, we'd all
be pornstars. It never comes back, because
it never leaves. Nice to smush you. Have we
made a nasty sound between us before?
A fist that grins would like to introduce
its help to you. I hope you can fake it.

LIFE OF CRYIN'

You did not break my heart, you just took a

dump on a tiny area of it.

You are the best kind of fertilizer.

You are the best kind of worst kind of friend.

We teach by being example students,

so I will not wait for myself to grow.

I will become Master of Ignorance.

A plague of doubt will vibrate across me.

You are a deep, deep, deep human being,

and I waste and waste my time, thoughts, and words

on you. I will continue to give you

these gifts, because my mind and heart are big.

I was born to be wasted, like a dog.

O Swine, I cast my bright pearls before thee.

I FORGIVE MY DAD

I forgive my dad

for not being there

when I had trouble falling asleep

and wanted him there

but he left and went back down the hall

before I could fall asleep

I forgive my dad

for not acting on his love

when I needed him

because the world was strange and new

and I didn't have the tools

to deal with it

I forgive my dad

for going on a date with his wife

when I had one night to see him

because the flight was delayed

and there was just the one night

and they hired a babysitter

I forgive my dad

for standing by while bad things happened

when I was defenseless and scared

because he needed to be cared for

by a person who didn't want

to care for me

I forgive my dad

for being a child whose parents died

when he was very young

and left him in a strange and new place

that he didn't have the tools

to deal with

I forgive my dad

for postponing or canceling his yearly trips

when I was a teenager in a faraway city

and anticipation was

a war across earth

that left buildings empty

I forgive myself

for my dad not being there

when I needed him

because he couldn't be there

because he couldn't forgive himself

for someone not being there for him

I forgive my dad

for never forgiving himself

I forgive myself

for not forgiving my dad soon enough

because now

is soon enough

AFTER DENVER

AFTER DENVER

AFTER DENVER

AFTER DENVER

AFTER DENVER

2020

DENVER

DADDY STATE OF MIND

Daddy is a state of mind

You can hate it, but don't lie

You may think I'm not old enough

But I'm not Chasin' the same things as you

Your eyes make it hard to tell what you're looking for

The Right Eye doesn't know what the Left Eye is doing

Boy, you need some Tender Loving Care

And you won't find it in Kansas City

You can be a kept man

Your daddy keeping you like the secret he used to keep

Or you can go to Whore Boot Camp

Get every shade of dishonorable discharge You can be

like me, kinky for loving the ungrateful

The daddiest trait of all

I've raised enough children today

I'm a Grandfather now—I'll spoil them

When someone tells you they feel lucky

You're then in a situation where luck is involved

All good luck eventually becomes bad luck with Time

So you might end up falling in love with loss itself

Death is what a Western Fool runs backwards toward

Remembering a future that never arrives

I'm a Silver Daddy ready to dismount into the Carnival of Ashes

When I pass through, nobody will be able to call me back

Men twice my age have called me daddy

But in truth, I'm nobody's daddy but my own

I've been my own daddy since my daddy left

Each morning when I wake, I think of what I have to do

Does being responsible mean blaming yourself for everything

How do you know which things to blame yourself for?

How do you know what your intentions are?

Other than notice what's on your mind, what else is there to do?

These are the four questions I ask my daddy (myself) today

And because I'm a good father

A great father with Time

I know to not answer them

When I fall in love with you, I fall in love with you forever

Your favorite person is the person who leaves you alone

I want to call him, but I can't

I'm his daddy, but I just can't call him

AFTER

DENVER, COLORADO

Gay men in Denver, Colorado

Gay men living in Denver, Colorado

Gay men living in Denver, Colorado, who made it their second home

Gay men living in Denver, Colorado, who made it their second home, having sex with each other

I was a gay man living in Denver, Colorado

I made it my second home, having sex with other gay men

Having sex with other gay men was my second home

Doing drugs and having sex with other gay men was my second home

I was living there

In Denver, Colorado

I did a lot of dishonest things in Denver, Colorado

I didn't answer calls from my mom, because I was working

I was busy working in Denver, Colorado

When I wasn't working, I was not alone most of the time

I was scared by my own behavior in my second home

I lied to my first ex-boyfriend about what I was doing in

my second home

My second home, Denver, Colorado

I learned from the best in my second home, Denver, Colorado

I drank coffee every morning in Denver, Colorado

I strung gay men along in Denver, Colorado

In my second home, I was a serial dater

I was surviving, but I wasn't living, said my best friend in Denver, Colorado

My best friend in my second home

I didn't have a first home in Denver, Colorado

I ate at Carl's Jr.

Qdoba

Chick-fil-A

Taco Bell

Taco de Mexico

Gladys Taco Tent

The Vending Machine at Trade

The Vending Machine at The R&R Lounge

Benny's

Racine's

Patxi's

Pete's Kitchen

Tom's Diner

Denver Diner

Sam's No. 3

Black Sky Brewing

Burger King

Chop Shop Casual Urban Eatery

Popeyes Chicken

Pepper Asian Bistro

Lechuga's

Santiago's

The French Press

Pudge Bros. Pizza

Blue Pan Pizza

Pizza and Grill

Bourbon Grill, that was my favorite

I would get the Bourbon Chicken with sides of Mac and
Cheese and Cajun Potatoes

My second ex-boyfriend's cocaine dealer was his friend

My second ex-boyfriend's cocaine dealer/friend drove
himself to the hospital in Denver, Colorado

My second ex-boyfriend's cocaine dealer/friend drove
himself to the hospital and had a heart attack

He had heart, lung, and kidney failure

He was put in a medically induced coma

This was over Christmas

When he was missing, I saw my second ex-boyfriend at the bar with his friends

They were worried

They were partying at the bar

This was in Denver, Colorado

I no longer live in Denver, Colorado

CUSTOMER

His name was Bob

He lived in an apartment diagonally across the street

   from the bar

He started coming in when I worked, seemed harmless

   enough

Mentioned he had a husband of forty years

He was a semi-retired consultant in his late 60s

He made a lot of money and traveled for work

He would usually come in within an hour after I opened

the bar, when there were very few or no other customers

He would pay for two scotch and sodas at once, $7, and

   tip $3

Sometimes he would tip $5 Bob became interested in my

   life

He asked me what I did

I told him I was a writer

He wanted to buy my book

I gave him the link to my book and he ordered it while

sitting at the bar

He friend requested me on Facebook and messaged me

"Please accept my friend request"

I accepted his friend request

He started messaging me on Facebook

He liked about a dozen of my posts in a row

The posts promoted my shifts at the bar, so customers

could know when I was working

I went to New Orleans to read at a hotel

Bob got my book in the mail and messaged me on Face

book

He was out of town

He brought my book with him

"I'm amazed by your poetry"

"I hope that picture in the back of the book is you"

I told him the naked picture in the back of the book was

me, that my ex-boyfriend took it when I was pissing and

I didn't know he took it, then sent it to me a few days

later

"You are so sexily handsome to me"

I told him I was glad he enjoyed my work

"I'm headed back to Denver"

"I'm on the plane telling the flight attendants about your

book"

"How did the reading go?"

"Did you read '150 Dollars'?"

I told him the reading went well, that I did read that

poem

The poem was about masturbating into a jockstrap and

selling it to a guy while working at a bar

I got back to Denver and resumed work at the bar

On one of my first days back, Bob came in

He brought his copy of my book and wanted me to sign

it, so I did

He grinned

"Are any of your poems autobiographical?"

You could hear the inside of his lips peel off his teeth

before he talked

I told him I sometimes wrote from experience

On a day off, I went with my roommate to the bar to

      pick up payroll

My roommate wanted to practice doing tarot readings

      on customers

Bob was there

She gave him a reading

When she and I left, Bob gave me a hug

"I love you"

I told him I loved him, too

I attempted to terminate the hug

He wrenched my face toward his and kissed me on the

lips

This is something Bob had started doing, telling me he

      loved me and kissing me on the lips when he said

      goodbye

Back at home, my roommate told me Bob's tarot reading

was "really dark"

He told her he was unfaithful to his husband for forty
years, and he recently got busted and had to
change his ways

He asked her if she read my book

She told him she did

He asked her if she liked it

She told him she did

"No, what poems specifically?"

"Did you like '150 Dollars'?"

"I like to think his work is autobiographical"

She told me he requested to follow her private account
on Instagram, and she blocked him

I told her he came in with his husband on a Sunday, the
only time that had happened, and his husband
made a joke about him being an alcoholic

I told her Bob once made a joke to me about poisoning
his husband

A few days later, I was working and my friend Cody was
there, drinking

So was Bob

Cody and I were talking about Twitter, showing each
     other stuff we found funny

When Bob motioned to leave, I didn't come around the
     bar to give him a hug

I told him to take care

He looked sad

Later that day, after work, I noticed Bob followed me on
     Twitter

I looked at his profile

He hadn't been active on Twitter for years

Until now

He started liking my tweets

Replying to my tweets

Messaging me on Twitter, quoting my tweets to me

He messaged me his phone number

"Share your number please"

I shared my number

I tweeted "Getting balls-deep in the tarot"

He replied "Show us"

I replied "Nope"

He messaged me "Ok was just teasing anyway"

At some point during this, my friend Jim told me Bob

    messaged him on Facebook

"Are you friends with B?"

He told him we were indeed friends

"I think he's just marvelous"

A few days later, I got a text from a number I didn't

    recognize

It was a picture of my coworker Chad—my "work

    husband"—in a funny hat

I texted "I love you" thinking it was Chad

The unknown number texted "I love you, too"

The unknown number texted a picture of Bob on a sofa,

    cuddling with a cat

I realized I wasn't texting with Chad

I texted "Oh sorry I thought you were someone else"

Bob texted "Oh haha"

A few days later, I was working at the bar

You'll never guess who came in . . .

It was Bob!

My favorite customer!

I was getting so lonely!

He told me he had just bought four more copies of my

       book

He told me they were for his friends

They were going to Puerto Vallarta for his birthday

They were all going to read my book

A little book club

"Wow, thank you so much"

"Thank you for your patronage to the arts"

"I really appreciate it"

About a week after that, I was working at the bar

Bob came in

Bob Frank

Robert Frank

My not-so-secret admirer, who lived diagonally across

       the street from the bar in an apartment with his

       husband and cat

He told me the books had shipped

"So you should be getting those royalties soon"

I thanked him for his patronage to the arts

He told me he was going to write a couple paragraphs
about each of his four friends, telling me about
their lives

Then, based on what he wrote about them, I was to
write a personal note for each of them in
the books

"You don't have to sign them as yourself "

"You can use your pen name"

I started laughing

I was nervous—I'll admit it

It seemed like Bob wasn't the greatest with "boundaries"

I told him no

He protested

"Why not?"

I shook my head

"But I want my friends to know I know the author"

I told him he could tell them that

I told him that was something he was doing for himself

"No way, Bob"

"There's no way I'm going to do that"

I turned and wiped down a reach-in cooler, something I
        had already done twice since Bob came in

He gestured with his hand, shooing the air, and stormed
        out, his first of two scotch and sodas he had
        already paid and tipped for left on the bar, 80%
        full

Bob . . .

I messaged Bob on Facebook

"There seems to have been a misunderstanding"

I catalogued to him what he had done

I told him it made me feel uncomfortable

I told him what he needed to do if he wanted to
        continue coming into the bar when I was
        working

"I will never come in again"

"You are so full of yourself it's preposterous"

"Barack Obama wrote me a personalized message in his
        book"

"As did Tony Bennett"

"Joan Rivers (rest her soul) did so as well"

"Who do you think you are to talk to me the way you did
    today?"

I blocked him on Facebook and Twitter

I blocked his phone number

Later that week, I was working on a Saturday

I didn't usually work Saturdays

Bob opened the door of the bar, saw I was working, and
    left

That's right, motherfucker

Yeah, you creepy, pushy bitch

Turn around, Bob

You can drink at home with your cat now

I'm not working for you for free so you can get cool
    points with your vacation friends

I bet they're dreading spending time with you in "PV"

I'm not a politician

I'm not a lounge singer

I'm not a stand-up comedian (rest her soul)

I'm not working for your vote

I'm not working for your applause

I'm not working for your laughter

I'm a writer

I don't make a lot of money

But my life is full

My life is beautiful

I work for nearly nothing, so rich, smarmy,

    scotch-swilling faggots like you can pretend to

    have emotional lives

Here's a new poem

I wrote it today

I wrote it just for you

It goes:

No

No

No

No

No

I'm glad you enjoyed my book, though

Thank you for your patronage to the arts

Hope you have fun in Mexico

Tell your friends

GAY POET HERE

Gay poet here, I write poetry and have sex with people
of the same gender

Gay poet here, I write poetry about having sex with
people of the same gender

Gay poet here, I have poetry and write sex with genders
of the same people

Gay poet here, I sex gender and about people with
poetry of the have write

Gay poet here, I people about and poetry havings with
sex of the write same

Gay poet here, I same sex with the poetry gender and
about people

Gay poet here, I gender poetry with sex workers while
shutting my dick in a vault

Gay poet here, I have I about I-ing I with eyes of the I I

Here poet gay, I hate people and the feeling is mutually
assured consent

People people people, people people people people
people people people

Anal sex dad, Jesus masturbated to the futures of getting
ass-martyred by a gay lion

Aye aye aye boy, fuck the poetry shut

Poetry identity politics, dramaaaaaaaaaaaaaaa

Here, I'm gay, and the ass leech has left the non-existent page

Militant mom gone, memory mooch metastasize

Short tall good bad, up down accident purpose

Starred Kirkus review here, my life is an unbroken creek
of moral grey areas

Shade: thrown; butt: fucked; vengeance: exacted

Stop reading this right now here, I stop reading this right
now and stop reading this right now with stop
reading this right now of stop reading this right
now

Fake twitter feud promotional tactic dead-eyed bored
wannabe bluecollar dad jokes

Gay poet here, I murder the edge of the universe to
nobody the moment for sleep

AHEM

Excuse me, but what are you talking about?

Shut up.

Can you please not do that anymore?

Seriously, stop.

Do it for yourself.

Nobody wants to hear you.

Not even you.

I can feel the outrageous effort of your pain so perfectly
it hurts.

I can tell you hate it as you do it.

You probably hate it most of all.

That's why you keep doing it, further and further cursing
any wouldbe recovery from it.

You can't want something you don't deserve, and then
get mad when you don't get it.

It's your fault for wanting it to begin with.

Think about it.

Why would you even want that?

Can you locate any foundation of your complaint?

Do you actually think you deserve anything?

Well, if nobody has told you yet.

If you haven't figured it out.

You don't deserve anything.

You certainly don't deserve this, but I'm feeling generous
        today.
A feeling, like any, that will pass.

You're lucky I care about you

.

This isn't "tough love."

It's actual kindness.

You're just so used to your orgy of discouraging niceties
        that it seems cruel and unnecessary.

Look.

I wish I didn't have to be the one doing this.

But somebody has to, because nobody else is.

My task here is grim and unsung.

It's like draining a portable toilet into a clown car,
wedging a rock on the gas pedal, and letting it
drive into a lake.

If you could just for a moment tear yourself away from
feeling slighted by an abstraction you created to
excuse your unearned attitude.

If you could just pay attention to what I'm saying.

Lord knows you've been demanding everybody else's
attention for longer.

It's my turn to talk to you.

Mine.

I am the pigeon that shits in your mimosa.

I am the mutt who lifts his leg on the lies you pad around
your life.

I am the friend you didn't know you had.

Here I am, friend.

A trinket in your palm.

You have my attention.

Go ahead.

Say your nothing.

Kick your legs that refuse to stand on their own.

Throw yourself down and scream it into your plush
pillow.

I am your pillow.

You're getting me wet.

Please don't get me wet anymore.

I'm wet enough on my own.

I bet you're so pissed off right now.

If you think I'm talking to you, I am.

If you don't, I'm not.

I am.

I'm not.

You can act like it doesn't matter to you.

But it should.

It will.

Don't fight it.

You can't fight time.

Yours has come.

YOUR FIRST EX-BOYFRIEND

I'm going to be your first ex-boyfriend

Most of your friends will become my friends

They will come to like me more than you

I'm going to be your first ex-boyfriend

You will try to keep tabs on me

But I'm not an internet browser, babe

You're an internet browser

You can rent a boy, you can rent a friend

But you can't rent a boyfriend—not really

I'm going to be your first ex-boyfriend

I'm going to make you feel wrong and dirty

But not in the way you like

The way you liked it when I berated you

Like a loving yet abusive father

We get hard for our pasts, as they harden in us

And hard as we try, we all smell like something

I smell like your first ex-boyfriend

I masturbated to you in the shower this morning

It was great, it was mine, because you weren't really there

You were never really there, were you, for me?

I remember what that feels like

I have a first ex-boyfriend, too

He wasn't perfect, but he was better than you

At least my first ex-boyfriend tried

Remember, after it went down (again)

When you said "I'm not perfect, either"?

Perfection isn't what I wanted

I wanted you to try, instead of trying me on, like shoes in the mail

I can only say "I'm sorry" for the same thing so many times

I can only say "I love you" so many times before you'll never know it

You thought, you felt, you thought you felt . . .

You thought you were falling in love, not tripping over

mine

I thought your thoughts held the truth

I should learn to pay more attention

I should see my mom more often

I should do a lot of things more often

You should do a lot of things less

It might be time for you to log off for good

And log in to your heart's wilderness

A place scarier than any real place

Is love a real place? I'm trying to find it

I've been there before, I gave you my map

But it's a conquest done on one's own

I'm going to be your first real X

You will be my last fake one

GRIEF FANTASY

I've been having this recurring fantasy/daydream

It's both of my ex-boyfriends meeting for the first time

At my funeral

My second ex has forgiven me for all the harsh, cruel,
      judgmental
things I said to him after he broke up with me, knowing
      that I was in a lot of pain, a lot of which he
      directly caused me

My second ex is sad, but he's not fully crying

My first ex is losing it, sobbing really hard, wailing and

whimpering, which is very painful right now for

me to imagine

My first ex has forgiven me for not being completely

truthful with him at times, at other times outright

lying to him, or lying to myself in front of him,

because I didn't want to hurt him

I was afraid of hurting him

He is crying like he cried to me on the phone when he

realized I chose my second ex over getting back

together with him, the first person I ever really l

oved squeaking in a way that penetrates me and

makes me think "I'm a bad person" / "I hate my

life" / "I want to kill myself "

They meet each other

They know who the other must be immediately

They say hello

My second ex is the first one that says hello and my first

      ex isn't really into interacting with him

My first ex told me he would imagine meeting my

      second ex and stabbing him in the throat with a

      broken bottle, killing him for taking me from him

Even though I chose my second ex over getting back

      with my first ex

My first ex loved/loves me so much that he blamed my

      second ex for something that I was responsible for

Because the pain of recognizing it was my fault was too

      much for him

That last line hurt to write

They start talking about me, and my first ex is resistant,

because he wants to just be with his pain and not

have to think about me with my second ex, but

he eventually breaks down further

He realizes that even though my second ex really hurt

me, he's not a bad person, and that if I fell in

love with him, that means I must have

seen something in him, and that he cared for me

They hug each other and cry

My mom isn't there

They are the only ones there

It's not a funeral

I don't know what it is

It's a forgiveness fantasy

They forgive me and trust that the ghost of me loves
        them and never wanted to hurt either of them

In the forgiveness fantasy, I can't forgive them, because
        I'm neither a ghost nor a spirit

I'm not watching them

I'm just dead

I've been fantasizing as if the only way my exes can for
        give me is if I'm dead

As if that will force their hands to let go

I didn't kill myself in the daydream

It was something else—something sudden and tragic

They leave the funeral that isn't a funeral and get drinks

They even laugh together, telling stories about how I was
a lovable idiot

Writing that last line felt good

They say they will keep in touch, because having a
relationship connects them to me

They become friends

I don't want to die before either of them die

I never want this to happen

I'm going to try to not die

I'm going to live as if they will someday forgive me

BEFORE DENVER

SLAB

Some asses were built by the devil just to haunt you. Aoudad, named after the Barbary sheep that roamed his oil-wealthy family's vast ranch along with a gallery of other exotic imported game they'd hunt, was keeper of the fundamental rump that left an indelible dent from whose negative slant of flesh I'd choose my future fucks. It wasn't long after I met him, and it might have been before or even at the same time we were introduced, that I saw Aoudad's bare soft divided push of orbs jiggle solid and pale in front of a locker row's glossy red grates still tacky from the multimillion dollar renovation his father funded for the school's football program, himself a former pro turned petroleum lord who had framed movie posters signed by celebrities in his mansion in the hills behind gates with the neighborhood name on them—an obscene degree of memorabilia shelved and locked on display behind sliding plate glass with signs that all had the same illustration on them of a hand holding a revolver pointed at its viewer that read: ain't nothing I got is worth your life.

No, it was all worth much more than my life, I'd think during team dinners hosted there, even though what the sign meant was if I took anything he'd shoot me, that none of his macho pop culture relics were as valuable as the life I'd lose for stealing one of them, a pair of gloves signed by the famous actor who wore them in the movie about a boxer, to name one. I routinely purloined cash from a box of end-of-day register till envelopes on a shelf high in the bathroom in the back of the pool chemical store where I worked, but I wouldn't dare swipe these tokens of a dominant life. Aoudad's butt was a shelf on which rested a priceless collectible, an object of infinite agony I'd die for even thinking about tickling past the fluid screen of his loving family, his rich daddy's guns. To reach the part of his body I wanted most, I would have to dig an underground tunnel, come crumbling up through the Sicilian tiles in his kitchen's bountiful pantry, pad by his father's private museum of opulent bro-kitsch, past the various rooms with sole purposes—the video game room, the pool table room—up the tall stairs, down the long hall, into his room, where there the plump bulk of it lay, its hard outline faintly perceptible in the dark like my own thief shape. I would have to dig a different manner of tunnel. I began to orbit him online.

The advent of social media coincided with my finding masturbation as one finds religion. I enacted the sequestered fervor devoutly, hourly upon myself, often with encouragement from the computer, though casual scenes from the locker room had already seized my imagination with ample carnal vibrancy to sustain my efforts. Even boys I presumed straight I saw glimpse Aoudad's prize while he changed and showered—it was that grade of marvel, an exceptional chunk of anatomy at which the butchest would gasp. I anticipated and planned my assward glances during those brief windows when the buoy surfaced in full from underneath the fabric, a sun hovering above—squeezed by to bulge—an elastic horizon, the red mesh shorts we all wore. It granted me the eyes of a cannibal. Aoudad must've known, been self-conscious of, its vulgar magnetism.

He was a year below me in school but we were the same age. I was young for a sophomore and he was old for a freshman when he first entered the JV locker room the spring off-season of that year. The coaches were preparing him along with other precocious freshman to play on varsity his sophomore year. He was the youngest of four brothers who'd all played football at East River, some of them going on to play in college, so he was a legacy there, the road already paved before him. I wouldn't make varsity until my senior year, which was standard, the status you earned after two years of pretending for the varsity team to be the opposing team they'd play that week, a duty called "scout team" where you "gave them a good look" of what they were to expect. During the period of the spring of my sophomore year to the spring of my junior year, I had very little contact with Aoudad, only speaking with him for reasons I'd half-fabricated, like asking to borrow his cell phone while waiting for rides in the parking lot after practice. I didn't have a cell phone, yes, but I didn't have to borrow his. I just watched him. It wasn't until the spring off-season of my junior year that we had no choice but to interact, being teammates and in the same locker room again.

Spring training involved a lot of lifting in the new weight room, of which Aoudad's father, Deets Ballast, paid for a large portion. Aoudad and I played different positions—he, a back, and I, a lineman—so I never got to spot him as he lifted, which was for the best, because had I stood behind him as he squatted, which in silhouette was some odd and rigid pantomime of sodomy, I suspect I would've either collapsed or burst from lust. Coach G, the defensive coordinator, told the team at the outset of spring training that he'd be selecting groups of us to travel to and compete in powerlifting meets on weekends. We all had to do it once and, as if to test my resilience in the face of a perfect temptation, one that could decode my longing to the point of total organ prostration, Aoudad and I were put in a group together.

Aoudad seemed gay—it should be mentioned—to myself and others. The matter of his appetite was a prominent murmur. His personality and behavior made a penchant for men all but undeniable. He had a high, bright voice and made pals with girls, mauling and pawing them non-sexually and sisterlike in the common area in conspicuous view of puzzled boys. His backside formed a mound on which his backpack sat. The glut of musclefat protruded twofold from his spine's end near-perpendicularly. The boys he hung around with also seemed to present as gay, if unknowingly, or immutably. I had no idea what they were up to among themselves, maybe nothing of imminent interest to me. I hadn't heard much of anything from anybody other than the most basic-headed speculation that even a stranger such as I had already made. I moved in circles outside the primary ones if not wholly on my own. I wasn't known for being a potential fag. I was known for being a weird person, a spaz, prone to outbursts, wild, crazed, hilarious at times, irritating at others, relentless, defective, puckish, moody, but not gay. Being bizarre was an armor, a camouflage, a diversion that, to me, just felt like living. That secret was nestled safely inside me like a slick, blind, baby eel.

But it's not as simple as not telling anybody you're gay. The "closet," a phenomenal term unfortunately suitable in its domesticity, is a behavioral structure, a carefulness that prevents acting on unlearned desires. It's something anybody can try to be inside of and anybody can try to assemble around anybody else. The closet is pretense. It's not exclusive to sex. Its functional scope is as wide and varied as desire itself. Anybody can live, or be demanded to live by cultural necessity, pressure, or coercion, dishonestly. In a dishonest and hostile world, practical survival isn't always an honest occupation. Often, it's a flat out fraudulent racket. There are gay people who are out of gay closets, yet still confined to others. Some never have a chance to be in the closet, innately deprived of the option of that special lie, ripped from any inkling or scheme of one and punched young. Some feel, and rightly so given their thorny circumstances, that at least part-time concealment is the only maintainable choice. To live honestly in any given moment means to face whatever may thrash from the punitive power of the fearful, confounded, bureaucratic, surveilled and self-surveilling masses. This, however, is not a "coming out" story I'm telling you, a person who is no longer here, so that's all I'll say about that.

SLAB II

At dawn on Saturday, our powerlifting group arrived at the locker room to try on singlets. We laughed because none of us had worn such things before—tight-fitting elastic blue numbers with thin shoulder straps that meandered low and showed our chests and backs. Slipped in one, Aoudad's form became pure abstract with real blood behind it at the same time—ham in shrink-wrap. It's hard to explain a bad, bad want, a vain groan no one can hear.

His friend since middle school, Mike M, a tall blond wide receiver who'd gotten his braces off recently and was a terrifying idea of a person-to-be, came with and from the start they were aloofly buddiedoff. You got the sense it was them two and then the lesser rest of us.

"Anybody bring honey?" Coach G said.

"Yeah," Aoudad said.

"Ballast! Is it the bear?"

Aoudad pulled a plastic cartoon bear-shaped container of honey from his bag.

Coach G laughed in a performance of fraternal satisfaction. "Freakin' awesome."

Coach G was an indefinitely extended version of a "super senior." He went to East River fifteen years ago, played football and won allstate honors both offense and defense. He attended college where he daydreamed of blitzes still, married a lawyer woman, moved back to a neighborhood like Aoudad's, became a coach. You could see him as both player and coach in the large team pictures that lined the hall outside the locker room, eyes squinting over a big jaw.

It had been said to us in the week preceding the powerlifting meet, during which it was made sure that our group was executing the various lifts with proper form, that a longtime custom at these meets, one at least as old as Coach G's time, was for the competitor to, in the moments before his lift, swallow a shot of honey. This was to spike his blood sugar and provide him with a surge of combustible energy. Coach G had said he would enjoy if someone not only brought honey to the meet, but especially if it came in a bear. This seemed like an important point of humor for Coach G. Aoudad delivered.

Transportation was a full-size yellow school bus with a couple dozen rows of brown vinyl bench seats, larger than it had to be for the few of us traveling to a facility in a more rural area. Coach G drove the bus like all coaches except the head coach were trained and required to. Our group sat in diffuse arrangement from just behind Coach G to the very back. I sat in front of Jorge, a guy I'd known and played football with since middle school but with whom I hadn't really bonded or become friends. He was the person on this trip I knew best, though, with whom I'd spent the most time on busses to and from athletic engagements, so we stuck together like Aoudad and Mike M, who sat next to each other across the aisle from us. I had my own seat like everybody did, lengthwise and stretched out, back against the side wall, head against the window, feet and calves hanging off the inside edge into the aisle. It was doubtful any of us wanted to be spending a weekend morning like this. It seemed Coach G was the only one of us who cared about powerlifting beyond the obligation of the affair, and he wasn't even doing it. Bench press, squat, deadlift, power clean, one ridiculous strain after another, tugs and grunts provoking bloated postures of heroic exertion. I harbored kinetics of a naked order behind the shared tedium of our semi-inescapable situation. We were deep in hill country now, the evaporating remainder of dew on roadside combinations of bluebonnets, paintbrushes, and wild grasses sparkling in a plane of flux. I slid my window down and hurt my eyes watching it.

We traversed the unfamiliar school's multipurpose gymnasium. Mats were spread across the floor and vertically condensable dark lacquered bleachers had been drawn from the walls for teams to sit and rest between their turns in the contest, which was already underway. This locker room was dank and rusted. We quickly switched into our strongman suits. Once clad, Aoudad and Mike M giggled and took pictures of each other with their phones, fracturing an atom of erotic hatred in my brain. They posed and made intimately silly faces for the lens. Aoudad arched his back in display. How funny and grand it was to them, the extent of his proud component. A pig-colored balloon God inflated. I could've chomped a hole in a cheek right then, climbed inside and died.

We returned to the gym and took our places in the bleachers. It was almost time for deadlift.

"Now might be a good time to break out the bear, Ballast," Coach G said.

Football coaches called players by their surnames, in excess, even if there was nobody else they could possibly be talking to, as a way of applying control. It smacked of militarism. You are named therefore you are had by me. The repetition insisted on this relationship.

The bear appeared and was passed around. Its lid was opened. Its clear body was inverted and pinched. Its sap was let into mouths.

We moved towards the deadlift mats. There were rounds where everyone had to lift the same weight, increasingly, until there was no one left. We all made it through the first and second rounds in our respective weight categories. Aoudad and Mike M were one category down from Jorge and I.

Before the third round of lift attempts, I walked over to Aoudad, leaned my head back and opened my mouth. He knew what this meant. I kept eye contact with him as he squirted in a golden portion.

"Good luck," he said.

I swallowed. "Now you."

He seemed to hesitate, but once I smiled, assuring him of the good-natured reciprocity of the exchange, he braced to receive the gift of substance. My grip got excited and I gave him more than his due of the saccharine deposit, the bear's black dot eyes never rattling from their hermetic trance. Aoudad gagged.

"Too much," he said.

"Sorry," I said, still smiling, "good luck."

I failed at my attempt. The honey could only invigorate the musculature that was already there. I went over to watch Aoudad with Coach G. The heave and clench made Aoudad dark red, almost purple, with a lattice of veins fattening around his face and neck.

Coach G smiled with his mouth open and held his hands above his head. "Yes, Ballast! Yes, Ballast! Yes, Ballast!"

Back in the bleachers, Aoudad and Mike M were giggling about something again. It was a girl with a giant ass. Given the nature of her attire, the whole border of its volume was presented. Though our group was exclusively male, this was a powerlifting meet for both boys and girls. Aoudad furtively took a picture of it with his phone. Coach G told him to quit it.

"Y'all could be related," I said.

Coach G contained his laughter. Aoudad blushed. He knew I was right. He knew they were ass cousins.

Back on the bus, there was a sense of relief that it was over. Aoudad and I were actually having a conversation. The hierarchy had been leveled, if temporarily, by this common experience. I asked him questions.

"Why do you play football?"

"I like it."

"You do?"

"Yeah, why?"

"You don't seem like you do. Do you believe in God?"

"Yes."

"Do you believe in gay marriage?"

He paused. "That doesn't really affect me."

What did he think, that saying he either did or didn't believe in gay marriage would've given him away, so he'd instead better abolish himself from the premise altogether? If I'd then had the nerve and wit I do today, I could've said, "So you're a career bachelor?" He knew I knew he was lying. He lied anyway. There's only so much recognition the constituents of a moment can bear if the fallout of that recognition virtually dooms them. He lied—poorly so—but he wasn't wrong. Gay marriage didn't really affect him. It didn't really affect me, either. It still doesn't, but I have a feeling it affects him now.

SLAB III

I was a glutton all summer, tangled in the lurch of a grudge, driven to the revenge of feeling something not yet felt, a feeling I anticipated and simulated that, upon integrating the warped regime of its memory, would mend the resentment of not feeling it. I wanted to sink my face into Aoudad's haunches like one of those padded rings at the head of the massage tables in the training room, to lap at the winking center of their grainy meadow, to taste past him, polish the floor through his taint with my tongue, plumb for undiscovered metals in a hidden mine, be the hook in the cum-mottled wall on which his taxidermal trunk was mounted. Fucking without complete spite wouldn't be fucking. It would be a righteous deceit. With controlled abhorrence is how you make a boy let you into him. You ac nowledge the devastation he is, and he thanks you, because he feels that more than what he's been told about himself in his life so far. Until you ravage him with your blessing, engorge him with your disgust.

This summer, I wouldn't be feeling something not yet felt, at least not libidinally, circling again and again through the rote framework of my yearning. I wouldn't internalize any healing experience, some liberating sexual catharsis where the usual guile of social life would come unglued, but instead would nurse in seclusion a festering device. There would be no spelunking for a seismic hell in the dark meat of a real man, only the invented but nevertheless compelling facsimile, the phonily pioneered-in-fantasy counterpart of what I wanted but couldn't bring myself to endeavor feeling, pushed deeper and more frozen into my desire, cemented there squirming. This was the summer I became a pothead.

In addition to the money I made working at the pool chemical store, I funded my loafing with the money I stole from the pool chemical store.

One weekend I was over at my mom's ex and his

wife's place. He'd bought me a bong for my birthday and let me keep it there, in his workshop. He headed project construction for a design-build commercial and residential contractor. He and I were smoking from the bong in his workshop in the late afternoon after I'd helped him jackhammer and remove a broken up bed of concrete from a room in his house he was renovating. The smoke we coughed morphed among the hanging tools and stacked equipment. His wife came in and took a hit.

"I think I need a nap," she said, "It always makes me so tired."

We were more hungry than tired from being stoned. I was giddy with exhaustion and slaphappy. We walked down his street to a fast casual Mexican restaurant and ate burritos, big ones we picked the ingredients for out of steaming and refrigerated metal bins along the counter as the employee compiled and rolled them to our specifications. I chewed just enough to swallow what I bit so I could bite again, to then swallow that bite, bite what I would then swallow of the tortilla silo filled with meat, beans, rice, cheese, salsa, lettuce, etc. I was still hungry, so we went next door to a fast casual Chinese food restaurant. K humored me, paid for my three-entree plate, shook his head watching me—red-lidded and shameless—push it in my face, a yawning trashcan. Yet I was still, if not hungry, desirous to continue eating as a pleasure unto itself, enjoyment derived from the very mechanics of it, so we went back to the fast casual Mexican restaurant and I ate another burrito.

"You can buy this one, boy-o."

I sucked it down like I was proving something to K and myself about myself, testing my capacity. There was an immense amount of pressure in my midsection now, which I clutched staggering back to K's place. I entered his workshop, this time alone, to get high. I took a big hit and coughed, pounded my foot and hooted raspingly, sat and stared at a nail gun recumbent on an air compressor in the corner. I saw Aoudad in my mind, his ass, in the locker room, the group showers naked, slick with hot spray, and in the commons covered by designer jeans with stitching on the back pockets. The unattainable vision throbbed its primal ware, transformed its look and texture, stretched its proximity as if responding to my attention. A bilious gloom surged forward in my abdomen and collided with a hollowness, roiled from the jolt. I fell to my knees and puked on the workshop floor, widely splattering the overeaten food. Breathing hard and sweating a lot, I cleared my scorched and corroded nostrils of the fragments that got diverted to my nasal cavity during the roaring evacuation. I wiped my slack lips on the shoulder of my shirt.

Through the glass in the workshop door I saw K's wife, up from her nap, approaching. She paused on the other side of the glass and I saw her mouth go "whoa." She came in and asked if I was alright.

"Yeah, I took too big a hit. I'm gonna clean this up."

"There's so much of it."

She was kind about it. I forgot my embarrassment as fast as I mopped. I felt better, empty, very high. I was looking forward to when I'd be alone later and could imagine what I wanted to, repeatedly and at length.

SLAB IV / V / VI

IV

I wasn't ready for two-a-days. That's a practice in the morning and another practice in the afternoon with a break in the middle to eat lunch and avoid the sun. Two-a-days started two weeks before and lasted until the school year started. The go-getters on the team trained over the summer, lifted weights and ran. I ate mint chocolate chip ice cream and jerked off. I was not a go-getter. The world was gradually teaching me a cumulative argument of what I was not, moving me into a place called "not knowing," where I would disappear and things would be noticed.

I can't go any further without telling you about instant messenger.

I'd found Aoudad's screen name listed on his social media account back during my junior year and began what I understand now as harassing him innocently enough in superficial pursuit of a friendship with him. Friendship wasn't quite the business I pictured, but it was the language I knew, the method by which I tried to access a language I didn't know. What I wanted was a mystery. It was a mystery to me that I wanted what I wanted, and what I wanted was mysterious and unfamiliar to me, but I also wanted mystery itself. Mystery was what I was after. It's what you're after, too, at this moment, both gone and here with me at the same time. Me, gone and here with you, gone and here with me. There was the world and there was the world. There was the world subject to the world, working to make the world to which it was subject, subject to it.

I was 100% the initiator of all correspondence. It wasn't that I didn't have shame, but shame can be displaced and hidden by desperation's swill. The contents of our conversations were general—just my light badgering of him that only ever extracted small talk designed to end fast—not memorable, except for one time, that was memorable.

I remember it well.

It started like any other conversation: I started it. *Wutangsword88* messaged *ABallast32*, and *ABallast32* messaged *Wutangsword88* back.

"hey aou"

"heyy [X]"

The normal vacuous banter. But then, after things strayed into a different kind of territory, perhaps from my nudging, he asked me.

"do you wanna jack off with me?"

What led up to this, whether the transition was abrupt or smooth,

I cannot recall with conviction. The gods of wasted youth, or maybe just waste, have it in their custody now. I might have asked him, straight-up and without preamble, if he was gay. He would've said no. But—he asked me.

"what? are you serious?" I said.

"yeah, it's not a big deal"

"but you said you weren't gay"

"i'm not, it's just a fun thing to do"

"I'm not gay"

"i know, me neither. it's just fun. you just jack off in front of each other and seeing the other person makes you excited"

"really?"

"yes"

"but where?"

"we can do it in the back of my car. i have an [SUV]"

"just park somewhere?"

"yeah after school"

He was a ginger, a redhead. A cup of white yogurt with flakes of dried blood in it. He'd sunburn easily so he had to wear a certain shirt to protect his sensitive skin during practice, on top of all the sunscreen. I was shocked and going insane it felt like. What a proposition. What a . . . trap? Was he setting me up for some public humiliation? I'd seen enough teen movies to have my suspicions.

"I don't want to do that"

I knew he knew I was lying. I lied anyway. The risk leveraged the mystery. I spooked myself. He abandoned the idea and it wasn't brought up again, except for when I brought it up.

Our rapport did change, though. I'd gotten frustrated with him growing a bit cagey after that and one night I ended up copying, pasting, and posting the entire text of his collaborative "rooting each other on" self-pleasuring pitch in the claustrophobic quarters on social media. I messaged him and let him know I did it.

"oh my god please delete it"

"why?"

"please just delete it"

"you asked me to do it though"

I toyed with him awhile, then deleted it. I don't think anyone saw it. I held the power, and then I let go of the power. It felt too cruel. But that power. It felt like a threat on my life.

V

Trouble came in ways of which I couldn't be blamed for being unaware.

I'd done two-a-days before the start of my freshman, sophomore, and junior years and each time got easier because: I got used to how bad it sucked a little more each time; the younger the players, the more the coaches tortured them with up-downs and wind sprints; I went through puberty and became more athletic. So this time around, with my place on the varsity roster secured by default, earned through my years of commitment and dedication to the team, I did nothing to prepare for two-a-days. Any senior could sign up for football––even if he'd never played for the team before, or ever before in his life––and he'd have a guaranteed spot on varsity. After three years of tolerating my voluntary disciplining for social reasons beyond me, my position in this red and blue world of supplemental fathers and birds that ran as fast as cars was the same as someone with none. Freshman, JV-B, JV-A, and Varsity. Pull down the stairs to the attic, retrieve the toys long in storage, play with the toys all night in wonder, and watch your best friend's dad whip him on his bare ass with a belt. You have earned your place.

I was pretty sure I wouldn't start this year. The offensive lineman who played my position in front of me had started last year as a junior after the guy in front of him's heart stopped during the second game of the year, a road game, just keeled over off the bench, the biggest player on the roster with a full-ride scholarship to a Division I school. He was resuscitated with an AED by a dad who happened to be a cardiologist, coming down from the stands to administer the automated current, clearing the body so nobody else would get shocked.

But everybody in the stadium got shocked. Both teams agreed to discontinue play. The guy ended up getting a pacemaker installed for a chronic arrhythmia and wouldn't play again. T-shirts were made proclaiming that now, it was for him. They were doing it for him now! Before, there were a disparate multitude of reasons why they had been doing it, but now, there was but one. The guy in front of me this year rose to fill the team's urgent need and started the rest of the year. Roused by their fallen comrade's spirit in tow, the team went all the way to the state championship game on a miraculous playoff run in which the entire community seemed to invest their souls. Then they lost. Salvation was avoided.

VI

I showed up to two-a-days out of shape. I wouldn't be starting so I didn't see much to be in shape for. Water breaks were mandatory so nobody got too dehydrated. We were told what hue our pee should be: apple juice, keep chugging, lemonade, better, clear, best. Late summer afternoon heat was the enemy. I'd witnessed minor versions of heatstroke in other players through the years but never in myself except for precursory symptoms. It wasn't like it used to be, players whose dads had played said. They said when players in their dads' day got dehydrated or heat exhausted, the coaches would put them in a room without light and have them eat salt tablets and drink water until the cramping, shivering, and dizziness subsided. Our training staff had tanks of water with several spigot hoses running from them. The water break whistles would blow and you'd shamble to the tank, your head cooking murkily inside your helmet, which you'd pull off by prying the ear pads apart and tilting it back so the pads would slide up the sides of your face, drink as much as you could without getting sick, douse your head to cool it off, spray the inner pads of your helmet to get the sweat and grease out. When you put your helmet back on, a nasty chill would wash over you.

The first practice wasn't in full pads—just helmets, shirts, shorts, and turf shoes. The field was artificial turf with a visible ridge halving the field end zone to end zone and gray metal grates surrounding for drainage. The field reminded me of the top of my skull, the crown itself also ridged end zone to end zone due to a narrow birth passage. But my head would flood. There was nowhere for it to drain. I waited for my face to leak and founder. The texture of the field was like rubber sandpaper—coarse and grippy, springy yet stiff with not a lot of give. If you slid and your skin made contact, it got ripped off and left enduring scabs. The field was a thriving Petri dish of staph bacteria. Skid wounds would frequently get infected, skin gnarled with red nodes pregnant with seeping pus. Maybe my brain had a staph infection, flooding its white knots from inside, out of nowhere, out of the hole that was me.

SLAB VII

I'd begun broaching the subject of my anality during this time. Aside from the occasional peeled vegetable, my main utensil was a toy maraca no longer than a marker with a blue bulb and black handle.

During the second week of two-a-days, when by then I'd been conditioned to them enough to indulge in the off-time, I pushed the maraca up too far in an especially adventurous session and it got swallowed and lost inside me. The round bottom of the handle slipped past the seal and I couldn't get a hold of its polymer surface with my greasy fingers—only brush the end. I tried to push it out like I would a stool, but the shape of it was such that it kept involuntarily getting pulled back in. I felt the grit shaking as I walked to the bathroom. I couldn't shit it out on the toilet either. I had to get to practice. I left for campus with it still inside.

Coach L, the offensive line coach, had us doing a drill that focused on keeping our feet moving during pass protection. We each partnered up with another lineman and took turns being the pass rusher. The idea was, if you moved your feet quickly enough while keeping a low center of gravity, it was harder to get around or bull rush through your blocking.

"Move your feet, [X]!"

My partner shoved me onto my back.

"Damn it, [X], what'd I just say?! Get low and move your feet or he's gonna put you on roller skates like that every time. Let's reset and go again."

Coach L blew his whistle.

"Chop those feet!"

The maraca's sand jiggled in rhythm. Coach L's command worked—I was doing a better job holding off the pass rush.

I heard the whistle again.

"The hell is that noise? What's goin' on—is one of

y'all bein' funny?"

The linemen looked at one another in merry perplexity and I joined them. My sphincter fastened. The maraca rose through my guts to my throat, then floated above my head like a siren of sin. Coach L grabbed the collar of my shoulder pads and pulled me toward him.

"What the fuck is this, [X]?" He snatched the levitating icon.

"It's a maraca, sir."

"A what-ka? How'd it get out here? You tryin' out for jazz ensemble?"

"No sir—I was using it to stimulate my prostate."

He released his grip on my collar, took a step back.

"Ah, uh—well, [X], that's very resourceful of you."

He put the maraca's bulb in his mouth and started sucking on it. He ruminated awhile, twirling the handle between his thumb and forefinger, the bulb rotating in his cheek.

"You know, [X], I've never seen a guy your size

move like you. Way I see it, there's no reason you shouldn't be dominating whoever you line up across from. Every play you gotta chop your feet like that."

"Yessir."

He yanked the maraca from his mouth while tensing his lips in a circle, making a wet popping sound.

"You're gettin' enough fiber I see." He winked.

The water break whistles blew.

Coach L slapped my buttock. The maraca shook. "Attaboy, [X]."

As I jogged to the tank, the maraca continued to shake.

THE GIBSON DAMNATION RESURFACES

I woke early morning on a continent of urine spreading to the edges of my in-laws' mattress. The piss, an acrid, whiskey-laden discharge that was unmistakably mine, had encroached upon my husband's side of the bed, dampening the areas of his skin that touched the flood released in sleep. The soak felt fresh and not yet tepid. The sheets peeled off my back as I crab-walked out of the brass California King frame, sloped crookedly onto the floor and into the lament of the present. He was innocent to the predicament, my little love buoy, anchored and bobbing unconsciously in a puddle of my blunder, his sweet, limp face for not much longer protected from the sourness of his—our—sopping world. I crawled around the foot of the bed, got on one knee like I was proposing to him this time, shook his arm.

"Peter——Peter wake up——I wet the fucking bed. I'm so sorry."

He snorted and rolled onto his back, making the linens squish.

"Hunnhn——"

"I got drunk and peed all over us, baby."

"What?"

Flipping over, he began to appreciate and fear his place of rest until he was alert and bewildered, frozen in a position like he was about to do pushups. He skittered laterally out of bed and stood beside me.

"We have to strip the sheets."

This was the first measure of an until now dormant routine for me. I spent my childhood under the iron gargoyle of this condition, hunched in office chairs while my parents had urological dialogues with specialists. Strategies were exhausted on my problem. I secured detector pads into the crotches of my underwear, snapped awake to a small alarm clipped to the sleeve of my nightshirt, sampled a motley of nose sprays and homeopathic remedies, drank from a jug of filtered water with prescribed minerals dissolved in it, expanded my bladder capacity, eased the struggle of keeping it in. Sleepovers, sleepaway camps, any overnight visitation outside the zone of my persistently soiled den was a waking hazard racked with anxious preparation and snookered by the unforgiving oblivion of dreams.

This was a new ordeal for Peter, though, who, after he helped remove the affected bedding and pillowcases and showered, initiated a plan to clean it all without his parents, who we were visiting for the winter holiday, finding out. Their bedroom was across the house from ours, but Peter said the washing machine, even though it was located adjacent to us, was too loud and would wake his nosy southern mother.

"There's a laundromat down the street. I'll go with you and get everything going, then you can wait there and switch it over to the dryers while I come back here and take care of——" he held his palms upward and pointed his hands down at the yellow abomination, "——this."

There weren't plastic sheets on this bed like the ones I grew up with, so my secretion accessed a moderate circle—the creeping perimeter of which was darker than the center—of the mattress. I imparted my technique to Peter of richly spraying the beleaguered region with an odor eliminator and aiming a hair dryer at it.

"I'm gonna shower before we go," I said. "I don't want to sit there smelling like piss."

The car stunk with the stained fabrics bunched in the backseat. We could smell it well now that we were clean. Peter drove, a cigarette drooping from his lips as he dodged a long pothole in the road.

"Don't look at me like that. I deserve a carton for this."

"I'm sorry, baby. Have as many as you want."

"You told me this hadn't happened since you were a teenager."

"It hasn't. I don't know what happened. I guess I drank too much too close to bedtime."

"Too close to bedtime!"

There was no telling the cause of the nocturnal

leak. The best explanation I ever got was it was hereditary. My grandmother and uncle had it, too, a fact I remember my mother soothing me with, giving the humiliation of my youth a membership. I discovered this about my cousin as well one summer after noticing the sleeping bag he brought to camp reeked like mine, disclosing to him our lineage's common woe. Welcome, Cameron, to the private alliance of Gibson pissers.

It was just Peter and I in the laundromat except for an old woman who didn't look up from her folding. We split the load, shoving the duvet cover and pillowcases in one machine and the sheets and mattress pad in another.

"Text me when it's dry and I'll come get you."

He left before I could thank him. I sat and watched the bulk infused with my flaw flop behind the pair of submarine-like windows—two more eyes rolling at my situation. The old woman delicately pinched the shoulder seams of a blouse and laid it on a stack of garments in her hamper. I imagined myself decades in the future as an old lady in a laundromat doing the daily washing of my pissy sheets. A calm swamped my sense of incontinence.

The drying phase stretched on due to the density of the items and my elderly role model departed. I texted Peter.

"How's it going? Almost done here."

"Same. I think I burned the mattress a bit."

"No you didn't. It's supposed to smell like that."

He picked me up. I held the warm pile in my lap.

"Wow, this feels really good. Very relaxing. It's kind of making me have to pee."

I saw him try not to smile, then give up.

Peter distracted his mother with details of the coming afternoon while I snuck in through the garage with the bundle. Rejoined in our room, I hugged him like a blanket I'd ruined and cleansed dozens of times. We turned the mattress over and remade the bed.

AFTER

MEETING

I got home from work at the bar and found a letter from my dad. It was the wrong address, but close enough to make its way to me. I had not seen him in over eleven years, not since I was a senior in high school. In the letter, he told me he hoped the letter found me well. He told me he was going to be in Denver. I lived in Denver. He told me my stepsister lived in Denver, and he, my stepmom, and two other stepsisters would be visiting her. She was getting married. Actually, she was supposed to be getting married, but no longer was, and they were all still coming.

The bar was not a bar yet. It was a construction site. I had been working there six days a week, purging, cleaning, painting, building, whatever they wanted me to do to help it become the bar they wanted. I got fired from my last job at a bar for calling out a few hours before my shift. I was having a panic attack and felt like I could not do it. My former boss texted me that we were done.

I found one of my stepsisters' email addresses on the internet and asked her what my dad's phone number was. I called him and left a voicemail. The next day, working at the bar, I noticed my dad had called and left a voicemail. I took a break, went to the alley behind the bar, which was shared with an office building, and listened to the recording of his voice.

I sat on the side of the office building's concrete entry and called him. He answered. He told me he was glad I got his number and called him. He told me his wife found my address on the internet. He asked me how I was doing. I gave him some updates. I went to school and finished. He told me that was great. I had been bartending. He told me he used to bartend himself. I was gay. He told me he had been around the block and was tolerant. I had a couple ex-boyfriends. He told me heartbreak was something he knew something about. My mom had early onset dementia. He told me he was very sorry to hear that. He told me I sounded mature. He mentioned I had blocked my stepmom and stepsisters on social media. He told me they wanted to keep those relationships alive, that it hurt them. He asked me to apologize to my stepmom and stepsisters. He asked me if that made sense. I told him it made sense that he was asking that. We scheduled a time to meet, late Sunday morning at a brunch restaurant four weeks from then.

The night before, I was up all night doing cocaine with my friend. I stayed over at his place. I did not sleep. A couple hours before I was supposed to meet my dad, lying awake on the couch, I got up, showered, and dressed. I walked west through Glendale, up Cherry Creek towards south of downtown. I walked up the sidewalk on South Logan Street to the restaurant. My dad was standing outside with his hands in his pockets. He saw me. We walked towards each other and hugged. He told me our table was not ready yet. He asked me who I thought was more nervous, me or him. I told him I thought he was more nervous. I told him I was more heavy-hearted than nervous.

We were seated by the host at a two-person table

in the center of a busy dining room. I ordered coffee and he ordered decaf. I asked him why he ordered decaf, and he told me he only drank one cup of caffeinated coffee a day, the rest decaf. There was a large, long table to my left with a family seated at it, celebrating a graduation. It was loud in the dining room, but my dad and I talked quietly.

He asked me some more about my mom. I told him more about what was going on with her, and he cried. He told me he and my mom were once in love, and that his mom died of a brain tumor when he was my age. He asked me about the bar, what sort of place it was. I told him it was a gay bar, a bear bar. He asked me what a bear was. I told him a bear was an older, full-figured, hairy man. I asked why my stepsister's wedding was called off. He told me it was because her fiancé was a drinker. He told me her fiancé did not have much of a soul.

After we ate and he paid the bill, I asked him if he wanted to walk around. He told me that sounded nice. We walked towards downtown. I brought up him asking me to apologize to my stepmom and stepsisters. He told me that was stupid and apologized. He told me he did not know where I was coming from. I went on and told him I blocked them on social media to protect my feelings, that the experiences I had when I was a child at his and my stepmom's house were hard, that I never felt welcome there. He told me he understood.

We kept walking. We were about to cross Speer Boulevard and enter lower downtown and southwest Capitol Hill. I told him about my failed romantic relationships. I told him both my ex-boyfriends made me feel like I was not good enough, but in different ways. They both broke up with me. He told me all the men in my life had left, including himself in that. He told me I was looking for relationships with men that reminded me of the feelings of the men in my life who left. He called it a compulsion pattern. He told me you can be aware of it, but it does not mean you can change it. He was a Licensed Clinical Social Worker. He worked with children. He told me when he was ten and his dad died, he blamed himself for it. He asked me if I was in therapy. I told him I had gone to a few appointments with people who took Medicaid.

We were walking north up Lincoln and about to pass the bar. I told him we were about to pass the bar. I did not want to pass the bar with him. He told me we did not have to if I did not want to. We turned and walked east through Capitol Hill. He asked me about going to school for writing, and what I was doing with my degree now that I was done. I told him I was a writer, that bartending gave me time to write, and that my first book came out this year. He asked me if he could read it. I told him I used a pen name and nobody in my family could read it unless they sleuthed it, which I would appreciate if they did not do that. He told me one of my stepsisters was a writer, too.

We turned and walked north through Capitol Hill, not far from my ex-boyfriend's apartment. I told him there was a park, Congress Park, where we could sit down. He was breathing hard and sweating. He told me he could not move around like he used to. Across the street from the park, I told him I imagined he felt a lot of guilt. I told him it was okay. I told him I was okay. It was fine. I was fine. He told me he did feel guilt. He thanked me for saying that.

We crossed the street and sat in the park under the shade of a large tree. People were playing soccer. He told me stories about my relatives on his side of the family. We talked about the state of the world. He told me stories about sports and asked if I still played. I told him I exercised, but did not play any organized sports.

He looked at his phone and told me he had to get going. He called his wife and told her he would be back soon. He handed the phone to me so I could talk to her. I told her maybe I could visit them on the East Coast sometime. She told me that was big, and would take planning. I told her goodbye. I handed the phone back and he asked me if that was awkward, then apologized.

He asked me where we were and I told him the intersection. I asked him if he had a car service application on his phone. He told me he did not, but could call a cab. He asked me how I was getting home. I told him I was taking the bus, that it picked up by the park. He called a cab. We waited and talked some more. The cab arrived. I told him I loved him. He told me he loved me.

We hugged. He got in the cab and left. I waited for the bus.

A PICK-UP ARTIST IN THE ANIMAL KINGDOM

I finished editing a poem and left Diane's house, in Edgerton, for RUFF'S, in Madison, a twenty-five minute drive, in her car. It had a hole in the front bumper, a box of Duraflame logs in the backseat. It was the end of January, a Friday. I had moved back to the area after eight years and landed with Diane, my old friend's mom. I tended bar at RUFF'S in my earlier twenties, which were about to be over in the summer. My last stint at the bar did not end well. But I was older, and a much better bartender now. I worked at a high-volume, destination bear bar when I was in Denver, from where I had just moved a couple weeks ago, to be closer to my mom, who was sick. The bar was called Denver Honey. Its logo was an emoji-esque bear head set on top of a paw with golden honey dripping from it. Yum! Woof! Arf! Grr! Bears, otters, wolves, pups and their handlers, leather daddies and their boys, and just plain gay guys—I had mingled with and served them all. I knew how to do it. There was nothing to it. I was a sometimes pleasant, sometimes catty robot behind the bar. My wit was honed. My honey was sweet. My body was covered in psoriasis lesions. A stress outbreak I was trying to get under control. I did not want to work in a gay bar again after leaving Colorado, but I texted Gino once I got to Wisconsin, to see if he needed help, because I needed help myself. I was on the ever-present cusp of broke-a-tude. He did need help. Help was wanted. He had opportunities. I had a stellar letter of reference from the owner of Honey, describing my "fun quarky" sense of humor. I was not just funny: I was subatomically hilarious. I wished he had let me proofread his letter. That was something I did on the side for extra money. I would have done it for him for free, an errorless letter being in my interest. I appreciated the gesture, though. I was grateful. I had no complaints. None.

Gino and I met over coffee across the street from

RUFF'S, before 69 he opened the bar. He had started tending bar three happy hours a week, he said, because it let him "keep track of things." He asked me what had changed since I last worked for him. I told him I had changed. I grew up. I was no longer resistant to posting about my shifts on Facebook, a sure sign of adulthood, which had always seemed to evade me in the past. He offered me a job. He said I could have whatever I wanted. I would take on some shifts, yes. Yes, Gino, I will work for you again. He was an older, stocky, grey-haired man of Italian descent with a beard like a genie's. He was somebody's type. Somebody I never wanted to meet! There goes that wit of mine. Up the river like a spawning salmon toward a bear. Grr! Chomp!

I parked on the street outside RUFF'S three minutes before 5, the start of my re-training shift, and dropped some quarters in the meter. I looked good. I had gotten a fade the other day to look the part. This otter's noggin was fresh, with minimal dandruff, thanks to some topical corticosteroids. I strode into the bar like I did not own the place. Gino greeted me.

"Did you not get a RUFF'S shirt?"

"Oh, I mean, yeah. You gave me one. It's in the rotation. Did you want me to wear it?"

"Well, yeah! Get one from downstairs. They're in the crates." Gino shook his head and rolled his eyes, looking to the full bar of patrons. What he was looking for in them, I knew not. Affirmation of his impatience and disdain for me, maybe. Just a guess.

"Okay, cool. Thanks, sorry. Won't happen again, sir. I'm just gonna hang my coat up."

"This is why you show up fifteen minutes before your shift."

"Oh, I just thought since it wasn't a shift change and I'm not relieving you—joining you rather—that I could show up when you told me to. I'm just gonna hang my coat up."

The back room was dark. I searched with my fingers for a switch.

"Why are you turning my bar lights down?"

"Oh, sorry, I can't find it."

He came over, head still shaking, and found the

switch for me, one of about eight.

"It's this one here on the top left." He flipped it and nothing changed. "Or I guess the top right."

The room lit up and I hung my coat on a hook. I opened the downstairs door.

"Which shirt did I give you?"

"It was the Pride one. The Stonewall fiftieth. The ringer tee."

"Get a different one."

I descended to the basement and the smell hit my memory of it. Reunited at last. Oh, how I missed you so, moist concrete. I found a different shirt in my size and removed it from its plastic bag. I shed the one I was wearing, a shirt with an angry-looking, open-mouthed bear's face on the back. Roar! The basement's cool, wet air soothed the rashes on my back. I put on my RUFF'S shirt, which was different—so very different—and went back upstairs.

"You remember how all this works, right?"

Gino patiently and graciously reacquainted me with the touchscreen point-of-service system above the register, an older version of Aloha, which is what I had used at Honey, except at Honey, it was the newest version. It was better. Better, faster, and sleeker. The one I was looking at was the same one that was there eight years ago.

"Yeah, most of it."

"Clock in using the last four of your social."

I started tending bar. The robot, which had been dormant for a long three weeks, had been activated. Its hydraulics wheezed and creaked. I greeted the patrons, some of whom I knew from my previous tenure there.

"You still drink Miller Lite bottles and shots of Jameson?"

"I switched to rum and diet, but that's remarkable," said Dean.

Dean-o was always my favorite. In a violent clash between Gino and Dean-o, if I was the judge——and I was——Dean-o would be the victor.

"Bryan, you like gimlets, yeah?"

"I'll be damned."

"Hey, I don't have to remember much. What about you? I don't remember your name but you do Seagram's VO and diet, right?"

"Yes!"

"What's your name again?"

We shook hands. It seemed like people were happy to see me. They were happy to have me back. Those I didn't know, well, they would learn. I would teach them.

"You ready for another? What are you having?"

"He'll tell you when he's ready. He drinks paper planes. I'll show you how to make one when he needs one," said Gino, leaning into me and lowering his voice, "we don't want customers drinking too fast. We want them to stay as long as possible. Helps keep the atmosphere of the bar."

The atmosphere, of course. What was I thinking? I knew how to make a paper plane like the patron's, which was almost empty, but I decided against mentioning it. I would not want to bristle any fur. Arf!

I went to give another patron a refill. He had a tall glass, so I made him a double.

"He drinks single talls," said Gino.

"Oh, my bad."

"Yeah, we don't want customers to get too drunk too fast. We want them to stay."

We wanted them to stay, but did I want to stay?

"Sorry."

I brought the patron his drink, a whiskey diet.

"Let's talk about these pants," he said, "they're a little baggy. We need to get you in something tighter. We need to get that shirt off."

"What, you don't like these joggers?" I spun around like a model, putting my hands on my hips and thrusting my elbows forward while sucking in my cheeks and making a pouty face.

"I'm just giving you a hard time." He laughed.

"Hey," I got closer to him, lowering my voice and tenderly touching his elbow, "I'd take my shirt off, but––"
"I need you to get some ice from downstairs and refill the cherries," said Gino.

"––Tell you about it later."

"What happened to the ice scoop?" said Gino.

"Oh, I left it in the well. Was that wrong?"

"Now you have to wash it. I don't know how you

did things in Denver . . ."

I washed the ice scoop, which had been made suddenly filthy by sitting in the very ice it was used to scoop. I grabbed the ice buckets from their hooks in the back. I went downstairs and filled them up, not feeling, at this point, in a rush to return. I filled up the ice wells. I looked for a glove to grab the cherries, but could not find one. This robot did not remember everything, after all.

"Hey, Gino," I apprehensively placed my hand on his back as he chatted with a patron, "sorry, where are the gloves?"

"Top of the stairs."

I put on a glove and headed to the cooler in the back, fished out a handful of cherries.

"Make sure to put the juice in there, too."

I flinched and almost knocked over the large container of cherries floating in their "juice." Gino was behind me, standing in the doorway of the cooler. The gay Italian genie had appeared.

"Yessir."

You will get your juice, Gino Bianchi. Worry not,

for I am your juice man. I am the deity of nectar. The otter of your loins. Mwah! I returned to the bar with the cherries, and the goddamn juice.

"Want another?"

I knew Dean-o did. He always did, until he did not. I made a single tall rum and diet.

"He drinks doubles," Gino said, "just assume our customers want doubles. We make more money that way."

I had done just that, just before, and was corrected for doing so. Which was it, singles or doubles? I was confused. I was so confused, in fact, that I was beginning to get upset.

"Here you go, Dean-o."

"Do you want a shot with me? Gino, can he have a shot?"

"No, he's training. He's on probation."

Jail sounded better. Lock me up, daddy bear. Slam the door. Slide me my food and leave me alone. I refilled another patron's drink, the one who drank single talls.

"That's a double," Gino said, "you poured him a double."

"Oh, I thought I poured him a single."

"No, you poured him a double."

"Very well."

All the liquor bottle nozzles had small weights inside them. Perfect pours. Exact pours. Nothing extra. You get what you pay for and nothing more. I remembered this from when I last worked there. Somehow, now, I hated it more.

"Dan-o is coming in, remember what he drinks?" said Gino.

"Miller Lite bottles and Jager bombs, right?"

"That's right. If you have it ready for him, he'll be impressed."

The Jagermeister was in a machine that refrigerated it close to freezing, with a convenient spout mounted on the front.

"Is the handle stuck?"

"You have to do it sideways."

"Oh, weird."

"Fill it to that line and fill the Red Bull to an inch below the rim."

"You got it." I tilted the spout handle sideways.

"Whoa!"

I let go of the handle. "What's up?"

"Oh, that's fine."

I brought Dan-o his beer and bomb.

"Oh, you remembered! I love you." He held my hand.

Gino, Dean-o, and Dan-o. I thought about it. Dan-o was Curly and Dean-o was Larry. Gino, without a doubt, was Moe.

Louis, the bar manager and a former coworker of mine, showed up to relieve Gino, who relieved himself at 7, two hours before the other bartenders. Gino was a man who made his own rules, as well as everybody else's. I gave Louis a hug. It was really good to see him.

I went to the bathroom, and when I returned, Gino was laughing, but not smiling. He was shaking his head.

"Hey, would you mind not leaving the Red Bull

cans in front of the door of the cooler, please, so I don't knock them on the floor and make a mess?" Gino looked at Dan-o knowingly, half-laughing, half-scoffing. Dan-o looked at me and frowned. He was on my side, but he was also in Gino's bar. RUFF'S.

I made a mistake. I had an accident. Whoops. I felt terrible about it. Nevermind that Gino did not see the can there, in front of the cooler door, before he opened it. It was my fault, and my fault alone. Nobody else was responsible for what had happened. Nobody but me.

"Clean this up. You can use a rag from the back. Don't use a white one."

I went to the back and Louis was there. I asked him where the rags were. He showed me. I grabbed a blue one, returned to the scene of the crime, and cleaned it.

"Which rag did you use?"

I showed it to Gino.

"Okay, that's fine."

I was glad it was fine. I just wanted everything to be fine. Gino clocked himself out and Louis took over.

"I'll have a tall Dewar's and soda with a single

shot in it," said Gino.

I made the boss his drink and he sat next to Dan-o. Another patron asked for a refill. I turned to Gino.

"Double, right?" I smirked, knowing how much I wanted to rip his beard out of his face with my fist. Grant me this final wish, my genie, so you may return to your lamp and be buried deep in Sicilian sands. Gino rolled his eyes. I wanted a cigarette, a habit I picked up over Pride in Denver, but I knew better than to do it while my overlord was present.

Gino finally left. The last hour or so of my shift with Louis went by smoothly. He and I worked well to-gether. It was fun. At 9, my relief showed up. He was someone I had never seen before. He was a balding ginger bear with glasses and a thick ass. The rare ginger bear, a weakness of mine. A thick ass, also a weakness. I was hav-ing a moment of frailty. He was adorable. I was smiling uncontainably.

"I don't think I've ever seen you before in my life," I said, "what's your name?"

"Tim. It's nice to meet you."

"It's nice to meet you, Tim."

I clocked out and sat at the bar, and Tim talked to me. We talked for five minutes straight. That is a long time to talk to a bartender. I was making him laugh. I could tell he was smart. I told him I was an artist, a writer. He told me he was a local politician. I told him that was really cool, and I admired people who could do that, because I could never. I told him I was looking for a place in Madison, and he told me he was connected to cheap housing resources, and could help me. I told him that would be great. I went outside and had a cigarette. I texted Diane.

"I don't want to work here."

When I returned, Tim was not wearing his shirt anymore. I was smiling. He was smiling. Smiles, smiles, smiles. I closed my eyes and looked down shyly, shaking my head.

"I have to go now."

I did not have to go. I did not want to. I wanted to talk to Tim. I wanted to look at him. I wanted to make him laugh. I should have left, though, and I did. Diane texted me earlier that it was snowing between Madison and Edgerton.

It was Saturday. I had the weekend off. My next shift was Monday. More re-training with Gino. I texted him.

"Hi Gino, yesterday was good. Thanks for everything. I can't make it to the event tonight. I know you wanted me there. Bummer. I was going to ask you for Tim's phone number. He said he was going to help me find a place in Madison. I'm going to create a Facebook profile tomorrow, by the way, to promote my resurgent role at the bar."

He texted me Tim's phone number. I texted Tim. "Hi Tim, this is Ben, your new coworker at the bar. It was great to meet you yesterday. I wanted to reach out, because you mentioned that, when the time comes for me to leave the boonies, you could direct me to some channels/ resources re: housing in Madison. Also we should hang out, if you'd like. You seem awesome."

"Thanks! Working right now. Gino mentioned he was giving you my number. I did a couple reach-outs since Gino told me a couple hours ago. If you're looking for a place right away, I know one person in town who has an efficiency available now through May 31st for 540. It's the off season, so a sublet is probably your best bet since it's almost impossible to get leases that start now."

"That's a good price. I'll need to work for a few weeks first. But something like that would be perfect. Thanks a lot!"

"Yeah I'll keep asking around too so let me know when you're closer to needing a place. We should totally hang out sometime too btw :)"

"That is what is up."

It was an hour before my shift on Monday, and I was dreading it. I had created a Facebook page on Sunday, and the bar friends rolled in. I was up to almost one-hundred already. I texted Gino.

"Gino, I hate to tell you this, but I can't work for RUFF'S, effective immediately. I'm not coming in this afternoon, or ever again, at least as a bartender (provided I'm not now 86'd for such a sudden departure). I've thought about it a great deal, and I know it's the right choice for me. I also know you will be completely fine without me. You've been fine and great for 14 years. I know such short notice is shitty, and I feel terrible about it. But I seriously cannot go through with this. I want to thank you so much for giving me the opportunity to return, but I especially want to extend my gratitude to you for talking to me about what's happening to my mom and everyone around her because of what's happening to her. I hope you're not *too* pissed off about this. It has to suck. I'm sorry. All Best."

"Ummmmm . . . ok! Did something happen to create such a major departure from where you were last week!?"

"What happened, happened within me. I love everyone at the bar. I just can't work there."

"Well ok then."

I deleted my Facebook. Tim texted me.

"What happened! No more RUFF'S?"

"No more RUFF'S. It was both a very hard and very easy decision to make. I'm going to tell you some things in confidence here, because I instantly felt a trust with you after meeting you. All it took was 3 hours behind the bar with Gino to know I didn't want to do it. But more, to ever work in a gay bar again. It's all I've done, pretty much. Right off the bat, he was on top of me and up my ass with criticisms, demeaning me in front of a full bar of patrons. He said I was late. I was on time. I make it a rule to show up early for shift changes, but I wasn't taking over for anyone. I was joining Gino to 're-train.' He criticized me for not wearing a RUFF'S shirt, as if one needs a uniform for that job. I told him it was in the rotation, that I just didn't wear it *that day*. He was not okay with that. It reminded me of everything that made working for him miserable. A customer nearly tried to suck my face off when he said goodbye. Another one, while I was smoking outside, tried the same. I was a very successful bartender in Denver. One of the most. I was beloved there. If you went there with me, and we went to a bar, you would understand and know this. It seemed Gino's primary goal on Friday was to humiliate me and put me in my place as his subordinate. But we all know who really makes bars run. It's the managers and bartenders and bar-backs and door-persons. The owner's authority is general, and s/he should entrust a dedicated staff with the details. But he's a micro-manager. He wouldn't let me breathe. He even said, when I left an ice scoop in the bin (an entirely normal and non-health-code-violation act), 'I don't know how you did things in Denver . . .' I'd have taken it jocularly with anyone else, but it struck me as definitively mean-spirited and cruel. It re-dawned on me just how humorless, grave, and arrogant he is at what he does. I don't like him, as a human being. Please don't share what I'm saying with anyone. Maybe you have a different relationship with him. He treated me like shit. I'm trying to move forward in my life. I just finished my second book the other day and I'm waiting to hear back from publishers. I have a skill-set and resume that exceeds any bar. I don't need it. I know the short notice was shitty, but he and everyone else there will be fine, barring minor scheduling inconveniences. I have other opportunities. Mickey's Tavern, for instance. Also I was really hoping I wouldn't develop a crush on any of my coworkers, and that happened last Friday when I met you, to both my delight and somewhat chagrin. I bet you saw right through me. I feel like I was pretty transparent. I'm not good at hiding in that way, or 'playing it cool.' You seem so wonderful to me, and I hope we can stay in touch, and even get together sometime. I'm not saying everyone should hate Gino or anything, but I can't permit myself to work for him. What can I say, my tolerance for him is thin, and I, a grown man, refuse to be treated like a child by another grown man. Also, 8 years ago he fired me by taking me off the schedule without any notice. I was 22. It cast me into hardship. So I don't have much sympathy for making the life he chose for himself any harder. I wasn't fired this time. Pettiness plays rough."

"You're not the only person to say that stuff about Gino. I have a good relationship with him but I also mostly started working again there just because he was low on staff. I know a lot of other folks have had different experiences. The RUFF'S community can be a bit much too sometimes. I did pick up on the other thing Friday though. You were a bit obvious ;). Shame too about RUFF'S. I was looking forward to running into you tonight. Celebrating my b-day :)."

"We can have a late celebration. Gino and I are done, but I have an intuition that you and I are not. Happy Birthday, Tim. You were the best thing about last Friday for me, by far."

"Thanks it's tomorrow, but I have to do forum prep and then stream a school board forum tomorrow so today is the day for celebrating :)."

"I feel it might be in bad taste for me to show up to RUFF'S tonight."

"Just a bit, it won't do you and Gino any good. He's good at reestablishing that customer-owner relationship though so don't bar yourself from coming back."

"I want to lay low anyhow. But I also want to go on a date with you, if you'll allow it. Even just to get to know each other more."

"If I'll allow it huh?"

"I mean. I'm just trying to be respectful. You're a politician. Yourwheelhouse is the concealment of emotions in the service of policy and representation. I'm an artist. I do the opposite of that. Hope you find that cute."

"I'd love to go out sometime. What's your schedule like?"

"(Checks calendar) wide open."

"What are you up to Wednesday?"

"(Checks calendar once more) nothing."

"Care to grab a drink? Since you mentioned Mickey's already how about there?"

"It's my favorite place in town."

"I like it because it's close to where I live so I can walk there :)."

It is Tuesday afternoon, Gino. Tomorrow, I am going on a date with one of your bartenders. I am pretty into him. He seems pretty into me, too. Did you know he has a pet parrot? He is a Congo African Grey. They both have the same life expectancy. Wild. I am looking forward to meeting him. Maybe Tim and I will come into your bar together, once you have cooled off. Are parrots allowed? I am not in any rush. You will not be able to do anything about it, anyway, when it happens. I am proud of myself,

Gino, for standing up for myself. I hope you are proud, too. I have had enough of the animal kingdom. I bet Tim found that attractive. Woof!

EPILOGUE

DOUBT DOUBT

You're not confident enough in your writing. Not like you should be. It almost makes me angry in an incredulous way. Really, it's like you're not confident that your life is interesting, on its own, as writing. Your life is imminently interesting, fascinating on its own. Just on its own. It doesn't have to be adorned with anything to make it amazing, because it already wholly is. I'm saying this because I've had this problem myself. I'm still constantly having it and fighting it. The solution that we create to this problem that doesn't exist is we try to make our lives in our writing more interesting with other things, because we feel like our lives are not enough. But they are enough. They don't need extra literary things to make them enough. In fact, the added, self-conscious work detracts from what makes our lives so interesting. We can't ever see it ourselves, because we're with ourselves all the time and can't get away. Maybe crowding our work with superfluous stuff to make what is already incredible and vivid and real more interesting is our attempt to get away from our uninteresting lives. But the entire point of this in the first place, the reason why I started at least, was to figure things out. Go more into yourself. Fully. We should become more of ourselves by writing, not less. When writing, it's not about thinking of something literary to write to make your life interesting. It's not thinking of what to write, it's remembering the thing itself better, harder, with the full force of your mind and heart behind it. Just knowing you're a good, worthwhile person. Being merciless with who you were. Because it's who you were, not who you are. Because you're a human being and you can change yourself. You've changed before and you'll do it again. I'm trying to change myself right now. I didn't write regularly for like a year. Who cares? That's who I was. Now, I'm a guy who writes something every day, because I know if I just do what I'm talking about, it will be enough. Enough to sustain me, fuck everybody else. They're lucky to know even a small part of my life. It doesn't need work. It needs less work. I need to tell myself this stuff all the time if I expect to muster the will to write. I have to constantly remind myself to stop doubting that my life is interesting and to step back and instead doubt the thing that is doubting that my life is interesting. Doubt that doubt. The mechanism of doubt. That doubt isn't you: it's everybody else. It's your distorted perception of everybody else, which we're always dealing with and having to let dismantle itself under the pressure of our frank gazes. It's about the quality and astuteness and unflinchingness of your observation of your life.

FEDS ON VACATION

POOKIE'S BLUES

I have Pookie's Blues

Let me tell you what that is

We were in bed last month

And I made up a song about him

Pookie's Blues

And we improvised verses back and forth

And made each other laugh

And the window was cracked

Because the building was hot

And it was nice outside

And it was nice inside

And it was morning

And we were holding each other

Singing Pookie's Blues

That's what I have

That's what I'm singing

It's a song I made up

And now I'm the only one who knows how it goes

And I'm not going to tell you how it goes

And I'm never going to tell you

Because I'm never going to be able to tell you

And it's not because I can't remember

I remember how it goes

I'm never going to be able to tell you

Because I'm the only one who has it

I have Pookie's Blues

ONE OF THOSE THINGS

Irrational fears viscerally linked to the egoistic guilt of loss

Guttural physiological responses of panic, dread

The imminent notion that one is about to be "got"

Triggers include

The sirens of emergency vehicles

The rumble of jet or diesel engines

The guilt issuing from one's psychological involvement
      in the figurative or morbid demise of familial or
      romantic bonds.
The dead lover or parent

Or both

Or friend

Your family chooses you, and then you choose your fam
ily, who still choose you

The people in your life

The emotional implications of your associative commit
ments

There are certain people

What can you say?

It's just one of those things

A LIFE-SIZE CUTOUT SHOOTING OUT OF MY BODY

In the weeks and months after my ex died, some of his friends' behaviors upset me

One wanted to inherit his sex toys

He also wanted to make life-size cutouts of him

"Party [his name]s"

I told my friend about it

"What does he want to do with them?"

Bring them along to parties, I guessed, so it was like he was there with him, sort of, though not at all

I pictured myself getting back home after driving all day—exhausted, still grief-stricken and cast about by persistent waves of shock—walking up the stairs to my apartment, awkwardly carrying under my arm a life-size cutout of my dead lover I'd put on the wall in my bedroom to watch over my long, sad nights

"Everybody grieves in different ways"

Another friend texted me a picture of herself in wine country sitting on a wooden fence, backlit by the setting sun—pronounced, elongated lens flares streaming in fiery spears across the frame

She said her friend took the picture while she was talking about him

She said it was his "light coursing through [her]"

"Hopefully it brings you comfort"

I wasn't sure what to say

I told my friend about it

"People are all so different"

No kidding

Was she suggesting she was a channel of his spirit—a Tesla coil of his lightning—his ghost shooting out of her body?

I considered trying to one-up her

Sending her a clearly computer-altered image of me summoning an eidolon of him

What she was suggesting was no less crazy than life-size cutouts, but it was more narcissistic

When you manufacture life-size physical representations of a dead person, at least the grief is laid bare, handled in a literal, if socially-misguided effort

The sex toys thing was just creepy

But hey

Everybody grieves in different ways

People are all so different

And hey

Nobody's death belongs to you

Hopefully it brings you comfort

NARRATIVE OF LOSS

I was on the phone with his friend

Who pounded on his door for minutes

Who said the hallway smelled bad

His friend called another friend

Who hadn't heard from him either

Who called a welfare check

An old you stacked on top of the new

Mess of self

What the ghost of learned judgments

Incessantly berates

Firefighters broke into his apartment

While we waited by the sidewalk

A knot of dread at my core

The paramedic cried more than I did

But she actually saw him

Don't be sad because it's over

Be sad because your narrative of loss

Is getting cleaner and more abbreviated

We filled out police reports

And were interviewed by a detective

Recording us with a body camera

Our trauma is mediated by an authoritarian state

(Hearing the most distant siren spikes my heart rate now)

And our state is authored

By our desire to control

Ourselves

Our narratives of loss

Our body cameras are recording

I didn't break down until I was alone

People have been posting

Reacting

Commenting

Wanting to know more

Memorializing

Saying who he was

When they met

How much he meant to them

How important they were to him (???)

How much they will miss him

How much will I miss him?

That is not a question I can answer

Until I've lived the rest of my life

And even then

He will be the only one I want to tell

Emotionally corporatized

We repeat-binge-watch our interior lives

Looking for Easter eggs

And forgotten cups

Looping back for clues

And answers to questions that aren't questions

But stories we tell to middle-manage an unruly love

We feel but can't understand

Lodged in the sickness of an impossible knowledge

Time clenches our teeth for us

Evicted from thought

What was I saying? My point . . .

My point:

Your life has a direction

But it's hard to know any more than that

FABLE OF A PERSONAL NATURE

I was an hour into the two-hour drive from the country to the city when he texted me

"Do you party?"

In contemporary gay parlance, that almost always meant meth

He texted some other questions

What did I drink?

What was my biggest turn-on?

"I don't mess with Tina—sorry can't text right now"

Cristina

Crystal

I had never

Though last year I had done a disturbing amount of co-
caine, but was avoiding that now, for the most part

I was attracted to him and was not going to turn around

He lived in an old building downtown

I typed in a code and he buzzed me through the front,
but a key fob was needed to use the lobby elevators, which
had gilded doors

I took the stairs and texted him from his floor's landing,
where there was another secure door

"Hey be there in a sec—just got out of the shower"

After a few minutes, he opened the door

He was sweating a lot

He seemed cheery, if nervous

He guided me to his apartment

"Wow, nice place"

"Sorry—it's kind of a mess right now"

"It's fine—it's not that bad"

There was a fair amount of clutter

He offered me a beer

"Thanks—dude you're sweating a shit-ton"

His hair was heavy with it—forehead, cheeks, and nose
covered in tiny beads

"Yeah, I sweat a lot—I'm also just really nervous meeting
you, I don't know why—you're really cute"

"You too"

We made out

His bed was vast and bare and there was a big TV on the dresser turned toward it with a gangbang porn playing

We sat on his bed and made out some more

I noticed a small monitor on his bedside

It appeared to be a live video of the other room of his apartment—the kitchen and the hallway to the front door—the one we had been in moments ago, directly outside his bedroom

"Is that . . . do you have a surveillance camera?"

"Oh yeah, I got that for free from this company I worked with at my job"

"Oh, cool"

"Plus, I've had guys over who've tried to steal from me"

"Oh shit"

"Yeah . . ."

We made out some more

"Hey . . . so you asked me if I partied"

"Oh yeah . . . sorry if that put you off"

"It's okay—were you asking me because you party?"

"Yeah, sometimes"

"Okay . . . what about now—are you partying right now?"

". . . Yeah . . ."

"Okay . . . so how did you . . . did you smoke it?"

"No, I put it up my butt"

"Oh, okay . . . huh . . . what does that do for you?"

"It just makes me really horny and it makes everything down there feel amazing"

"Does it dissolve?"

"Yeah . . . it takes like fifteen minutes"

"Is it all dissolved now?"

"Yeah"

We had sex

"I've never done it before, but I kind of want to try it"

"Yeah?"

"Yeah—but not putting it up my butt—do you have a way to smoke it?"

"Yeah . . . is it weird that it really turns me on that you've never done it before?"

"No—I mean, I can see how that's exciting . . . wanna set

me up?"

He pulled a water pipe/bubbler from a drawer in the corner

"Nice rig"

"What?"

"That's the same thing as a rig—you do dabs out of them, weed"

"Oh"

He dropped a crystal into the small hole at the top of the glass globe and handed me the rig

He lit the torch and held it beneath the globe

Smoke began to fill it

He gestured

"Go"

I exhaled

"Oh wow, this is . . . wow"

He hit it and put the rig back in the drawer

"Wow . . . this is . . I can see how this is so popular"

I was at once at home in the speed

Its high was pure and clear

He tapped a few crystals out of the bag onto his belly, plucked one up with his fingers and put it up his ass

He put the extra back in the bag, but there was still some finer residue on his belly

"What do you want me to do with that powder?"

"—Shhh"

"Sorry"

"My neighbors can hear me—the walls are thin"

"Is that why you have that sound-proofing?"

"Yeah, they've complained to me through the wall before"

"Oh . . ."

Whispering, he instructed me to lick my finger, pick up the meth dust with it, and put that inside him

He injected lube up his ass with a syringe to help with the dissolution

We hissed our words and waited

I looked at the gangbang porn playing and it occurred to me that most of the guys seemed to be high on meth

"You know who I always thought Adam Russo looks like?"

"Who?"

"Shel Silverstein"

"Oh yeah, he kind of does, that's funny—he's actually been over here before"

"Adam Russo, in your apartment?"

"Yeah"

"Damn, wow, how was that?"

"He's really cool—you're super easy to talk to"

"You too"

I started eating him out uninhibitedly

I tasted something extremely bitter

I realized I was licking meth around his asshole that never made it in and dissolved

It was getting me higher

I was crazed and animalistic, groping and slopping on his body parts

My life was miserably out of control

I loved it

We had sex for a few hours, getting high periodically

At one point, I was having trouble getting hard again, so I took two Viagra that he gave me

There were points when my heart was beating so hard I had to take a break

On our backs, chilled with sweat, talking

He sat a bit more upright and held still

"What's up?"

"I thought I heard someone at the door"

"Oh . . ."

I looked at the monitor on his bedside

Grainy footage of the other room of his apartment,the hallway, the door

We put clothes on and went downstairs and outside his building so I could have a cigarette

"Why are you living way out there in the country?"

I told him

"I'm sorry, that's awful—my mom is actually showing symptoms, too—my sister and I want her to go to the doctor"

"It can be hard to bring up or get anybody to do any-thing about it at first, including yourself"

He ordered a pizza

We talked more and I had another cigarette while we waited for it to arrive

I could not finish a slice, but managed to drink a glass of

milk

I told him I was going to leave

"I thought you wanted to spend the night"

"Yeah I know, but I can't sleep"

Driving back, I caught a glimpse of my face in the rear-view

My eyes were big and glassy

My cheeks were flushed

My skin felt tight and weirdly rough

Just outside of town, right before dawn, it got hard to see

I tried to blink, but could not anymore

I was barely able to pull over and had no choice but to leave the car running before slithering into the cold, wet grass

QUEER'S DECONSTRUCTION

After Black Thought

I grab the mic and make the crowd say "get off stage

faggot"

in stride I'm undeniable I'm all the rage faggot

a pale sage faggot, they played stale gadgets

in an exhibition primpin' for a male pageant

I embrace frail faggots, swillin' ale faggots

still-in-jail faggots on a box spring mattress

clinically insane faggots, who twist the vein ratchet

givin' head in a waterbed or on a plane faggot

I'm such a lame faggot, I'm so ashamed faggot

I'm Freud's boy-toy, I'm an aberration faggot

no I'm dynamic, yeah, always changin' faggot

not a kitchen television simple ready-made graphic

that's Will & Grace faggots, aim your brain past it

come unnamed, I'll put it simple and plain faggots

turn the page faggot, your soul ain't plastic

blow it out the faggot frame, fuck a corporate game

faggot

I can see you're in pain, don't be afraid faggot

don't just behave passive, get up out the shade faggot

and if you can then grab the reins and have a little faith

faggot don't remain tragic you don't have to be the

same faggot

it's a new day bright like a blade hatchet es-

cape from a straight-jacket let 'em play catch up

high salary or minimum wage brackets

when you die that's all you're gonna you get paid faggot

check it out here's a new way to "gay bash" it

hear the siren it's an incomin' air raid faggots

I know it seems amazin', but I swear it ain't magic

everybody's strange there's no one in the world to
blame faggot

I am such a crazed faggot

no I don't need your praise faggot, take back what you
gave faggot

image cataclysm of an arcade labyrinth

watch my back turn away: can you hear the rain laugh-
in'?

I'm passionate, yet have nothin' to lose or gain at this

I am not a tame faggot, hope you're entertained faggot

I give a military captain a lapdance

make him crap his pants in a tantric panic

O yes I'm howlin' at the moon you better get a good
gander

eat your fruit and vegetables, serve you like spoon han-
dle

you eat fish for the crude acid, I'm a harpoon addict

boom for real, I'm not a cartoon faggot

ancient statesman, but not Pericles

the basement's where I yawp barbarically

gettin' pecked by this rock hard parrot beak

come through smellin' like stockyard kerosene

(inhales sharply through nose) yeah I'm a pungent fag

in the corner suckin' hand-rolled London shag

come through wearin' nothin' but dungeon rags

just to incite a riot like thunder stabs

please I hope you can understand

that I've seen more shit than a plumber's hand

here come a voice from another land

to just hit your head like your mother's pan

DODGEVILLE (INTERLUDE)

I'm not planning on moving to a city

I'm in Dodgeville

I'm not trying to find love

I'm in Dodgeville

Where they ride motorcycles on Thursdays and park them in the lot out back

I'm in Dodgeville

Where they fry fish on Fridays at the bar and church

I'm in Dodgeville

Where they sell popcorn on Saturdays at the single-screen
movie theater

I'm in Dodgeville

Where you'd be a fool to miss the Sunday meat raffle

I'm in Dodgeville

Where I fuck the fat mayor in his big house and never
spend the night

I'm in Dodgeville

Where I'll be for the foreseeable future

I'm in Dodgeville

You should visit sometime, but not uninvited (I have a
gun)

I'm in Dodgeville

It's actually a pretty cool place, when you're not a little
bitch about it

I'm in Dodgeville

It's actually really nice

I'm in Dodgeville

There's nothing to let go of here, when you just stop

WHERE HAVE ALL THE BULL DYKES GONE?

After Paula Cole

[Intro]

Cum, poo, pee, whore

[Background singers]

(Sci-scissor, sci-scissor, sci-scissor, sci-scissor)

[Verse 1]

Oh, you give me heady

In your shitty fixed Chevy

Why don't we just bitch, scowl, and be grave?

Spread your hand in my wide cooch

Give me a little brine smooch

Like the skin of old fish fillets

[Pre-Chorus]

I will be real grumpy

If you withhold my pills

[Chorus]

Where is my mom's pain?

Where is my big strap-on?

Where is my frugal spending?

Where have all the bull dykes gone?

[Verse 2]

Why aren't you gay and queefing?

Wear slacks and pack the pee-pee

And I'll sit my little bum on your meat

Oh, you know my snatch squirts

Uncorking on the mattress

How will we get the stains out the sheets?

[Pre-Chorus]

I'll help raise your children

If you cheese both my gills

[Chorus]

Where is my mom's pain?

Where is my big strap-on?

Where is my frugal spending?

Where have all the bull dykes gone?

[Bridge]

I'm wearing my Labrys tonight

But you, but you won't throat my V

Spread my fat thighs

Spread my fat thighs

Spread my fat thighs

[Verse 3]

We finally sell the Chevy

When you're discharged from the Navy

And you took that job in the Twin Cities

My split ends look like yarn

Munching this chicken parm

Almost every single day flick my bean

[Pre-Chorus]

I will nosh the fishes

Please just don't call me queer

[Chorus]

Where is my mom's pain?

Where is my big strap-on?

Where is my frugal spending?

Where have all the bull dykes gone?

Where is my Gertrude Stein?

Where is her slimy chum?

Where is my lonely anger?

Where have all the bull dykes gone?

Where have all the bull dykes gone?

Where have all the bull dykes gone?

[Outro]

Yippy-I'm, yippy-gay, yippy-I'm, yippy-gay

Yippy-I'm, yippy-gay, yippy-I'm, yippy-gay

Yippy-I'm, yippy-gay, yippy-I'm, yippy-gay

Yippy-I'm, yippy-gay, I'm-I'm-I'm, gay, ga-ga-gay

SOLICITED PATHOS

I spoke with my aunt on the phone for an hour

My mom's organs are starting to slip

My best friend broke up with me

I'm a bad friend, self-absorbed to the point that I don't show up for others

My aunt told me not to be too hard on myself

Then told me I was in denial about my mom's illness for years

She told me it was happening when I was a teenager

My mom and I lived alone together

I've edited this poem 307 times

But it's still good

I don't know what to do

My aunt and I talked about how sometimes denial is not knowing what to do

You know something is wrong, but you're afraid to address it directly—name it even

Sometimes not knowing what to do is the only thing you can do

It's the only thing you can do right now, isn't it?

HOW TO SPOT FEDS IN ART SPACES

Little to no information upon drawing a background report

It's pretty easy to scrub the public stuff

That also means that person went to that length to do that

Private early schooling—Montessori, Waldorf, etc.

The Bay Area

New York

International parents

Being a giant shitbag weasel all-around

Controlling art is a key element of social control

It's really easy to wipe your history

It costs money or time, but is very doable

Feds aren't necessarily feds, per se

Most people are already doing what the state wants

Unwitting CIA/FBI interns

During MKUltra, the CIA made remote-controlled dogs by implanting electrodes in their brains

That was over a half-century ago

Use your imagination

It's all you have

Qualities of character that signal the presence of under-cover federal agents in art spaces:

Creates division while labeling others divisive

There is so much more

Records you without your knowledge or consent

Promotes and glamorizes/romanticizes drug use

Chain-smokes cigarettes in public

They declare the need to meet in parks

They want to talk through group drama

They say we are all friends

We are not friends here

Some of us definitely aren't "comrades"

They discredit women's suspicions as hysterical

Intimate partner violence is a leading cause of death among women (especially younger women)

Courtesy of GoonInc., this poem is called "How to Spot Feds in Art Spaces"

This is goon propaganda

This is art-action

This is a psyop

An ever-changing, dynamic, intuitive cartoon forcefield of infectious, viral enlightenment, joy, darkness, and truth

90% of media consumed is owned by 5 corporate conglomerates

When culture industry interests try to co-opt and neutral-ize it, we've already switched to something different, so it can't be captured

You can't capture freedom

You can't fight peace

Guerilla/Viet Cong style psychic disentangling and reformulation

No identifiable system or method

They take over leadership roles and then take unexpected trips

They need to see stuff still got done the way they wanted while gone

They take people camping

They talk about the least secure shit but insist they "understand security culture"

They use either woke or anti-woke language

They have the ability to host at a gallery

They always have the best locations (not great locations)

They want roommates

They have a big house a self-employed/freelance artist could never afford, with not quite enough roommates

They never say they want to work with cops, but bring

into the space people who suggest there are some good cops

But they hate cops

But they know so much about cops

They have reporter/journalist friends

They work for media companies

They ask too many questions

The less information, the more creepy and suspect

The arrogant thrill of deception smirk sociopaths display

There are cops on the payroll and volunteer cops

People like this are never as smart as they think they are

Closing ranks upon being identified

Make a loud noise and see how everybody scatters

Mysterious deaths

The most effective way to do a hit on someone is to make it seem like an accident/suicide

The families of these fucks are important, too

There are CIA and FBI families

There are neoliberal families

There is intergenerational wealth at stake

Kingdoms of violent theft, based on nothing

Foundations of insubstantiality

Gelatin molds

The artifice of greed

The innovation of innovation

The progress of progress

Delete all your social media

Don't fuck around in the metaverse

They map social networks in virtual and real life, in spectacle and on the ground

There are publications/websites that, in semi-coded, semi-subliminal ways, make political/ideological/religious espousals on either side

These exist to identify and collect, distract and control people in a meaningless culture war paradigm that ignores reality

Dark Money

Honeypots

I hope the NSA enjoys the humorous conversations I have with my friends, while they eat Chinese takeout before their ridiculous, bloated machines

I bet they feel bad they're going to have to kill us with invisible lasers that cause illnesses

As long as your dissent stays within a cultural simulation, you're not a threat to power

Occupy was infiltrated, hijacked, pulled in a bunch of different directions, and eventually broken

A lot of feds aren't even aware of other feds involved in the same infiltration

Black Panthers, Oklahoma City Bombing, etc.

Major American events that shifted the mood

People asking if you are "operational"

Data is available on anyone—the subversives have been tracked

It's a tragic shame, the price of trying to actually challenge powerful, evil shit

It's enough to make any rational, normal person give up and just try to live their own life, which is what they want

Resigned by/with instrumental reason

Not everybody has the option of giving up, though

The biggest threat to the powers that be is a truly free person who has accepted their death as a consequence of that struggle

If enough people did that and exposed the truth, they couldn't stop it

I get emotional thinking about it

(Keeping in mind "they" is "us" and vice versa at any given moment)

But yeah, the Rothschild family is going to drop a tornado on my grandmother's house

You are already dying

You are focused on your career

You are gardening

A librarian no more

Every self-employed artist is a threat to the system, and 2 out of 3 are actually the state

Gain knowledge of firearm safety and practice hand-to-hand combat

They come out of nowhere and steer the narrative toward the mild-mannered

They use either professional or "street" claims of credential

Their backgrounds won't seem real at all

Their dads are ghosts

Ghost = absolutely no internet trail to them about anything

Client work

Foreign copyediting

There are no real-life artists who never had to do real jobs, W-2 based work

Over-the-top LinkedIn profiles

International art dealers

Cruise ships

Instagram

Not real

Avatars

They—

Chain-smoke—

Cigarettes—

When you call them out, they deflect by accusing some-
one unrelated of something unrelated

Gaslighting the whipped

Ghostriding the dick

Grief as currency/social capital

Memorial as humiliation ritual

Trauma ballin'!

It's been a wild last 10 years of culture wars

They are total scrubs and chumps

Sheriffs of Fuckingham

Unironic emoji overuse

Phantom senses of humor—the suggestion of laughter without its realization

These motherfuckers are GLOWING with it

Shake the tree without showing your hand

They take over spaces for professional gain

They put your name places without your consent

Acknowledgments

Connections that aren't there

They plan in advance and will tell you about it

Exclusive nonprofits, neoliberal bootlickers

They act like fools

I'm not the crazy one

Be wary of who you talk to about this

Someone close to you could be a collector

Someone you respect and admire

Don't let your trust be so easily seduced

A baiting operator may try to reach out to pump you for
information

They fabricate experiences in their lives, recreate ones
that closely mirror your own, in order to strategically

ingratiate themselves to you, and on the pretense of this false bond thereby gain your social allegiance

Empathy siphoning, sympathy mining

They want to talk one-on-one

They want to "chat"

They are sloppy and weird

They boast of "making moves"

Their bosses are pissed

Is it me?

Am I operational?

How can you know?

That's how it feels

I came out of nowhere, and to nowhere I will return

Substance use to cover infiltrator guilt

The short game, the long game

The top floor, the ground floor

Fake conspiracies, real conspiracies

Operation Mindfuck

"Subversive poetry"

The one true tell:

Is their art actually good?

My daddy issues are in the stars

At least that checks out

Be honest with yourself about what you really think and feel about what you directly observe

Don't just stand behind yourself and think about your thinking

Reducing the public risk of the surface presentation of your thinking to others

Don't defer to the looming shadow of qualitative or moral relativism—the feigned neutrality of consensus group-think—in either art or action

You are the final authority of your experience, and it's your choice to grant it to others

There are people capable of thinking and acting in ways beyond your comprehension

They will say you're being paranoid/insane

But this happened, happens, will happen again, and will continue to happen again

Shit is about to go down

Animals before a storm

There will always be a new variant

There will always be a new cosmic object

So you better be ready

I am joyful and defiant

The world vibrates darkly

I am fucking hilarious

Anytime anyone does anything cool, someone else is
there to Andy Warhol a whole generation

The fundamental question:

Can you produce good art AND be a pig?

Having an imagination isn't enough

You have to actively use it while testing its ideas critical-
ly against the history of empires and their subordinate
peripheries/proxies

The prince is safest on the throne immediately after being
shot at

Fuck fascists

F'sho

They are here with us right now

I see you

*

Feds—false prophets of the new millennium—I stand in total merciless judgment of you

Celebrity artists, publishers, editors, agents, critics, influencers, podcasters—the modern priest class

The world has become a miserable wasteland because of you and those like you

You who make a vain, sick mockery of life

Who are you to mock this one, great, and only life?

You are nobody to mock this life

This life both you and I are

This precious human life that will never return again

This life that is the life of all beings

This life is nothing to mock

You will bow your head in sorrowful shame and lay your-self prostrate before this life for how you have failed to live it

This life is all you love and fear

You will love this life, and you will fear it!

YOUR LAST REAL BOYFRIEND

I am your last real boyfriend

You are not reading this, because you are dead

Your friends fished your big shirt out of your laundry for
me

I held it to my face this morning and cried, while also
aware of how *Brokeback Mountain* it was

And vain, like everything your last real boyfriend does

A ridiculous thing to call myself, even lyrically

I got cathartically drunk with your devastated brother
this week

Who confirmed what you told me about your dad

Damn girl, you were not exaggerating

I am so sorry

I told your brother I was the closest thing to a boyfriend
you ever had

He told me you criticized his hair plugs

Bitch, he had cancer

I told him the last time we spoke on the phone, you told
me I had abandonment issues

I know, mister

Just because you know something about another person,
doesn't mean you have to say it

They probably know already, and you're just being mean
and insecure

I remember telling you, in bed: "I know what it's like to

be a twisted, knotted-up person"

You cried

I know you

Can I tell you I am relieved your suffering is over?

Can I tell you I am angry at you for putting us through this?

For somebody who could make me ashamed at will, you refrained most of the time

I know what it's like to carry shame with you like an organ

To see shame merge with desire

To be aroused by what you are ashamed of—to be aroused further by that shame

If you can't eliminate it, you can at least pretend to control it

But nobody is in charge, even of their fantasies

I am your last real boyfriend

And you are a real person

And you are worthy of love

And you did not live like you knew that

And you knew that

And I loved you anyway

And I love you

And I miss you

And I don't care if nobody else thinks loving you was
worth it

Because they didn't see us together

We were bad for each other

We were good for each other

We were not perfect

We tried to heal

You were a bad boyfriend, which you admitted

You were a good friend, which I am saying

Your last real boyfriend—I don't want that title

I want to see you again

I will erase everything

My books disgust me

I want to meet you for the first time

I want you in your car, saying: "I'm going to kiss you now"

Before kissing me

And driving us to your place

Which has been emptied out by your family

Which will be rented to somebody at a higher price

Your dad wouldn't go any lower than 5500 when he sold your car

He opted to have you cremated, because it was cheaper, even though it's what you wanted

Even when it's nobody's fault

You have to take responsibility for something

I'm sorry I snored

But I'm the one losing sleep now

Your last real boyfriend

Your first ex-boyfriend

Your first real boyfriend

Your daddy, your beautiful boy

I still can't believe it

But what is there to believe?

Things are known over time

And you have nothing to be ashamed of

MEADOWS

My aunt and I saw my mom at the assisted living and memory care home for dinner. The staff can't control her enough to where she's not taking up too much attention from the other residents. She's constantly standing up and sitting down, removing clothes and shoes and socks and putting them back on. Stripping in front of people, reaching into her pants. She's nonverbal a lot of the time and will repeat what you say to her. Muttering to herself. My aunt told me she was saying "my dad is dead, my dad is dead, my dad is dead, I'm going to die, I'm going to die, I'm going to die" the other day. Her dad died ten years ago. She was breathing shallowly and anxiously. She's on Seroquel and Klonopin now. She didn't quite know who I was, I don't think. She was confused and compelled to do something and couldn't rest in the moment and breathe. She's lost a lot of weight and has difficulty eating. Her hands were shaking. I tried not to cry. At one point she looked at me and told me she loved me, and I told her I loved her too, and cried. I walked with her to her room, holding hands. She kept telling me she loved me. My aunt and I stayed with her awhile in her room, the door to which had her name posted on it with a colorful hand-drawn background. Hallmark channel on the TV. I sat in a chair at her bedside and held her hand while my aunt lay with her and sort of cuddled. She closed her eyes and I said how exhausting it must be for her. My aunt got up to leave and my mom asked if she'd be there tomorrow, and she said she would. I stayed with her and got in bed and held her hand and kissed her and told her I loved her so much and she told me she loved me. I tried to be calm and in the moment with her. I got up and told her I was leaving and I'd be back tomorrow. I kissed her and told her I loved her and left. She's about to be moved to a psychiatric hospital for geriatrics where they'll try to change around her medication so she's not so restlessly agitated all the time.

Her autonomic nervous system is breaking down. Digestion, motor skills, spatial awareness. Love, fear, being calm in the moment. Ham sandwich, fries, canned fruit. The home may not accept her back, depending. I have a feeling she'll die in the hospital. I wish I could talk to Brian, who was my boyfriend, who died almost eight months ago. His mom died of this. Brian is dead, Brian is dead, Brian is dead, I'm going to die, I'm going to die, I'm going to die. I'm going to rest in the meadows of this moment.

BEYOND
BEYOND

BEYOND BEYOND

BEYOND

BEYOND BEYOND

BEYOND

BEYOND

BEYOND

BEYOND

CELL THERAPY

I'm peeking out my window

My relationships are getting more complicated

I just want to grill chicken thighs in peace

Without getting ominously circled by a tweaker flashing
        TikTok from the driver's window of his Geo

I just want to smoke fenty mids in peace

Cleanse the nation with smoky bangers

K-9 units smell me and my friends states away

We refuse to travel with sauce

The wind picks up (the dirt) where it left off

The pines tremble for an open field

The blackening clouds scramble across the federal sky

I write a poem at the hotel bar because I'm a federal mess

The G23 is in the trunk, disarmed

You can keep the roll of duct tape

Because my friend and I aren't adhering

So bump that

We're not seeking shelter

We're not seeking asylum from anything

We're okay, we have enough power to live, and you're
    going to let us grill, smoke, and pass through in
    peace

Because that's how it must be

Because we're neither seeking nor tweaking

We have books and snacks, asshole

We have dollar-store waters

And won't be spiritually detained

PASSWORDS AND USERNAMES

My grandma took care of my mom until a couple months before she died, when she was placed in an assisted living facility. They couldn't handle her, so she was placed in a geriatric psych ward with 24/7 observation and aid. They were authorized to give her stronger drugs. My grandma lived through the Great Depression and was trained as a nurse. She felt guilt about handing her daughter over to the care of others.

I haven't thought about what happened in the geriatric psych ward much. It was an austere, technological, grim, peaceful setting. Windows looked over trees and a lake, powerlines and industry. This place, the final physical station of people whose minds are being taken away from them. Plaque-thinned fat. It's hard to pretend to know another's perception, and impossible at the stage my mom was at. But there were things that indicated ideas. She rarely spoke. She said "no" a lot. We sat in front of the TV together. I ate food while melted ice cream was poured into her mouth because she couldn't swallow anymore. She said "I love you" to both family and nurses, gave us hugs. I hugged the nurses, too. When my mom would cry and seem scared I would hug her. Sometimes she would push me and others away, struggle to break free. One time she was walking down the hallway with the nurses and I was walking toward her, and she saw me and started crying and held her arms out and I cried and held mine out and we embraced while the nurses cried. I'd sit next to her in bed. The nurses told me to take care of myself. I wasn't sleeping hardly at all for weeks. People were worried about me. I would stay at my grandma's at night because I didn't want to be alone. I told my mom "I love you and whenever you want to go you can. I'm going to be okay, because you were a great mom and did a great job." Her face relaxed and she smiled a bit. I wasn't sure I'd be okay.

We'd walk in circuitous routes along the halls. I let her lead the way. She was in charge. That's what the nurse said. I agreed. The nurse also said my mom was hallucinating the smell of smoke and saying "fire" in a panic. Reaching her hands into the space in front of her, manipulating invisible objects. Saying "I want to go home." The nurse said home wasn't a house, but eternity. None of us are home. Or we are but don't know it yet, can't until we leave the first and final human station.

My friend drove out to be with me during what would be her last three days. He got into town earlier than I expected, while I was on a walk. He picked me up along the sidewalk in front of the cemetery and we proceeded to hang out and have a really good time. We ate the fantastic pot roast I made, which he watched me prepare in pornographic awe. We sat and talked about all kinds of things. I can't even really say. We walked around town, played darts and pool at the bar. We laughed a lot. We visited some of my family. He gave my grandma a painting, a female nude that made her blush. We went to dinner with my aunt and uncle, who he loved. We went to an outdoor range. I remember feeling I'd be okay. We were cleaning the guns at my apartment and I got a call that my mom's breathing had changed. She was close. My friend packed his things.

I drove to the hospital, about an hour away, and was greeted by my aunt and a nurse when the elevator doors opened and told my mom passed before I got there. They said it happened thirty minutes ago and there was no way I could've made it in time after getting the call. I went and spent time with the body, the eyes that looked at nothing, the hanging open mouth breathing nothing. She was home. I was not. Or I was but didn't know it yet. Couldn't until I left my first and final human station. I left the room so my grandma could be alone with her daughter. I stood outside the half-open door and heard her say "I'm not ready for you to go."

We ate a meal at a bowling alley after. My grandma said "It's been sixty-eight years of doing the wrong thing." I didn't have it in me to disagree with her, but next time I see her (it's been a while), I want to tell her that when you're helpless to awful things greater than yourself, which is almost everything, almost everything feels like the wrong thing. The Great Depression is over, but the Fate Discretion is yet to come. As it always will be. A lot of anything can happen in a couple months. I'm writing this by hand in a notebook my grandma had, to help remember things. It says "Passwords and Usernames" on the front cover in her handwriting.

WHAT HAPPENED YESTERDAY AND TODAY AND TOMORROW (I BECAME THE NOBODY OF MYSELF)

I woke and read a text from a guy I'm seeing casually. "Fuck, I'm so horny right now! I want your fat cock deep inside me so bad shooting your fucking load deep inside me." Above the words, an over-the-shoulder picture of his ass, back arched, making an intentionally cute/awkward face. While I appreciated the nature of his message, it also made me apprehensive, because, though we have fun and exchange a great deal of affection, I don't foresee a committed partnership for us, something I do foresee him wanting eventually, because, well (gestures towards obvious appeal of self). If you want to be my boyfriend, you can't react to and comment on YouTube videos aloud at my apartment while I'm doing the dishes. I'm going to think you're talking to me. You can't like "movies with a strong female lead." Even if you just want to be my friend, there are certain things you can't do. You can't keep a "shit list" in your fifties, or meticulously plan, catalogue, and rate on a calendar everyone with whom you've had sex. The neurotic, hysterical clinicians of our corruption—passively and vaguely and noncommittally offering bureaucratically sterile barbs to the rote atmosphere, while always (being ever half-assed of spirit) giving themselves an out, a disclaimer. Maintaining every empty connection without connection. Lecherous and treacherous, another facially edited soldier in the demon nation of unchecked motivations. What do you actually want (do you even know and can you admit it)? Is there something I can help you with?

Over time, there are things you notice in people's personalities, certain inclinations of mind manifest as behaviors, particular cultural patterns, that have deeper implications about values and intelligence, or a lack thereof, despite expressed, broadcasted politics. Usage of the word "ally." Invoking "accountability" within a pettily deranged personal revenge subtext. Wearing a Carhartt ballcap and growing a nasty grey beehive out of your chin because your voice is gay. Just be gay with your gay voice. Belt out blue-collar showtunes with some lost twenty-something's yam in your gnome bussy. Mentor him in the ways of narcissistic Gen X resentment. Trad, atheist, queer, normal, punk, a witch. I don't care what you want me to know you are, based on whatever mass-produced, mindless group option was made for you to which you agreed or are recoiling from, and now compulsively spread. Stay away, and enjoy the maintenance of your shit list while you slurp your shit soup and make yourself sicker and sicker. You're too old for what was never cool in the first place, and I'm old enough to know when an older person never grew up. But no yeah, you're totally cool/badass, and anybody who thinks you suck is jealous and wrong.

Knowing myself well and already feeling a little touchy and temperamental (zooted off that Gorilla Glue nlah), I decided to do laundry in a different town because the mat in mine gets goofy sometimes. People getting out of windowless vans with logos of defunct businesses painted over, wearing pink dresses, velcro sandals, big antennaed transistor headphones. Christian propaganda magazines on the coffee table, traveling workers eyeing me. Freakish behaviors exhibited by a new class of semi-melted people—one who wouldn't have survived what my grandma lived through, one who will perish within a couple days when the lights go out (unlike me—haha!—who will last up to a week), despite the woodburning stove they regularly need to remind everybody they have while their polywife fantasizes about having sex with a guy she works with at a quaint, rural grocery store. Karma's not a bitch. Unless you mean the projected, prideful willed actions of a psychic landscape's vanity. It's kind of like publicly sacrificing your newborn to Satan. If you make that deal, just be ready (God forbid you act surprised) when it comes time for Him to collect what you owe. I was born in Boston, can read minds, and am afraid people are following me.

I entered the smaller, quieter laundromat carrying a black plastic garbage bag (clothes), a white kitchen bag (bedding), and a container of detergent for sensitive skin (I'm sensitive). An older woman in a scooter immediately greeted me by my name. Not remembering hers but intuiting it was a family friend, I said it was good to see her, while feeling a creeping auguring of something like the embryonic, visceral notion I was experiencing the pre-beginning stages of the brain disease that killed my mom, surely wrought by the drugs I no longer used, like Facebook accelerated hers. My teeth are falling out.

Okay but so—the lady, the woman who knows my grandma. I'm talking to her. Are you with me here? I'm talking to the woman in the wheelchair thing at the laundromat in the town other than mine because it's supposedly more chill and there's not scary people who want to mess with me there. My aunt mentioned this to me. I explain all this to my grandma's cripple friend. "She was right, this place is super cool actually. These machines've gotta be from the eighties, seventies even. They were built to last. And they're like half the price as the new place. It's so quiet here. I heard sirens in my air conditioner last night. I mean, I mistook some of the sub-noises within the din of my A/C for sirens, like an emergency. But then an actual siren passed by outside and I could tell the difference, so that was good. I have PTSD from my boyfriend dying."

"Oh yah . . . the only thing is you gotta be careful not to come here at certain times. These old ladies get very protective of the machines they're using. They get mean."

"Whoa, sounds intense, thanks for the tip. My grandma called me delicate the other day."

"Oh that's so cute! It's usually Mondays Tuesdays and Wednesdays during the day."

I feed the change dispenser a twenty and over two trips carry in cupped hands more quarters than I'd need and set them on top of the washing machine. A triple loader. I rip open the black bag and shove in my dirty shit. Clothes, towels for the hands and body, cumrags. It smells like a bevy of cyborg doves. I set the water to hot with double wash cycles (nlah). At some point, another woman comes in. Fat with a short haircut and a lot of makeup. My girlfriend, basically, my dream wife. She stations herself on a chair in front of a wall of dryers. Loadstars. My boyfriends, basically, my dream husbands. She's scowling at a washer across from her post. "Look at those clothes just sitting there. People just leave their clothes in the machines. Other people need to wash their clothes, too."

"Oh yah, I think she went to the gas station."

"So inconsiderate."

I watch my clothes and towels and rags get sloshing, then scout for a smaller machine for the bedding. I behold one even larger than the triple loader. The beefcake. The big daddy. Maybe someday, but not now. Putting my bedding in there would be like. It would be like putting something way too small in something way too big, you know what I mean? I go around by where the fat woman is, finding a machine of perfect capacity.

"That one is the one you should've used, if you didn't have

whites. You could've done 'em all in one."

"Oh yeah, the big daddy. All my clothes fit in the triple loader, though. I actually wash the whites with the darks in a single batch, on HOT. Haha, betcha thought I had the colors in the black bag and the whites in the white. It's actually my bedding in the white. *[Smiling at my grandma's friend while the fat woman looks displeased]* I'll inadvertently dye my garments pink, but I won't mix in the bedding. I don't really give a ding-dang but I draw the line there know'mzayne-nlah."

We share a chuckle and I'm pretty sure she farts (oh shih haha nlah). I snort while ripping the white bag open and shove my bedding in the machine I chose to use and get it sloshing, like something sloshing in a thing. Sloshy slosh slosh-ola. Literature. Lyricism. Lilacs on a locomotive in Lancaster. Is your motive loco? Autofictional divorces, sub-stackedly rendered. *[Making hateface]* Oh yeah you like that?

I throw the ripped bags in the garbage and place quarters in the laundry bag dispenser, which eats them. No bag. Seventy-five cents, and no bag. So inconsiderate.

"Did it just steal your money?"

"It sure did *[demonstratively slamming the metal coin receiver on its track, reaching hand up inside dispensing mouth]*. There's no bag."

I walk over to the ladies, arms folded, pretending to be in a huff. "Maybe I spoke too soon about this place. Some of my friends on the East Coast who almost kill themselves working in factories on the computer. They work with food, too. Ew! Any given day, seventy-five cents is all they have to spend on their t-shirts and books and raw denim and boots and jewelry. That's not nothing."

"Oh yah, that's just awful."

"Yeah this country is coming apart at the seams, and it's all because of religion, science, history, art, and deepfake A.I. tech that, in conjunction with foreign infiltration at all levels of every institutional system (academic, justice, medical, social, financial, industrial, etc.) real crimes can be staged and covered up, and innocent people can be framed for crimes they never committed, hell, things that were never crimes in the first place. Nullified damnation, fabricated evidence. Throw in a little rhetorical values-leveling nihilism, blended with pious crackpot eternalism on the other extreme side of thangs, and you gotcher self a cute lil recipe for a collapse necessitating a great reset towards a globally consolidated and streamlined government."

"Oh yah, I love a great human harvest and culling perpetrated by elite homesteading non-entities. Can't wait for these quantum comps, too. Nlah. Did I do that right?"

"Absolutely. AND I just threw those bags away. Not that I would've used them."

"Ya know, I actually have a plastic bag in the backseat of my car. You can grab it if you want."

"Zomygot. That's very sweet. But I couldn't. Oh wait. That reminds me. At the risk of sounding low-IQ. Haha I just realized this, but I actually just bought black plastic garbage bags and tall white kitchen bags (with drawstrings for ease nlah) at the Farm & Fleet before coming here. Like right before. They're in the back of my car. I can't believe I didn't think of that. Not the ones I used to bring the dirty stuff in. The ones I just bought. Those can totally be used for clean laundry. Just because they're not branded as laundry bags doesn't mean I can't use them as such. It's all just plastic right. I deserved to have the seventy-five cents stolen from me [pointing finger at temple] space cadet! But also . .

. umm . . . lifehack much? [Excitedly looking at fat woman, who looks disgusted].”

“Wait . . . YOU have a CAR outside?!”

“Yeah, haha why?”

“[Looking at my grandma’s friend] I just figured someone dropped you off here [rolling her eyes like ‘THIS bozo . . .’].”

“[In overly proper tone] No ma’am I’m fully capable of driving myself places. [Smiling at my grandma’s friend] But no yeah someone dropped me off from the asylum. The shuttle pulled up and they let me out the straitjacket for the afternoon haha.” We share a laugh and this time I fart, relieving the completely uncalled-for tension created by the fat woman with the topographical makeup. Dark green-yellow toxic smoke billows from her ears as I realize she looks like Wario in drag. WAAAAAH! NLAAAAAH! I leave to grab the new bags from the car, farting again on my way out, overhearing the fat woman remark on people from where I live coming to where she lives to do laundry. These . . . invaders. My mom grew up here and went to high school a few blocks away.

I'm waiting for my laundry to finish washing. My grand-ma's friend leaves and says goodbye and I say take care. Scanning the community corkboard, I see a poster advertising job positions as a meat cutter. Childish? Maybe I'll become a meat cutter. Nah I'll never work with food. Ew! The fat woman goes "yeah I need to use three dryers."

"What's up?"

"I'm going to spin them for just a few minutes and then hang them up at home."

". . . Right on."

My clothes are finished, so I shovel them into a metal basket and roll it over to a Loadstar just beyond the edge of where the fat woman is sitting. I dump the clothes in—the colors, the pink-whites, the towels, cum everywhere—I get it spinning and flipping, because this is a new kind of short story, written in a new grand style that is delighting and amazing to some (open readers), while confusing and angering to others (dangerously obsessive closet cases with crumbling home-lives, mommy-cop therapists, jilted acquaintances, resenticrats, etc.).

While I'm waiting for my bedding to finish, I open one of the smaller dryers and check it out, make sure it's good to go, and the fat woman goes "put your sheets in here when they're done [pointing to one of the dryers she's sitting in front of]."

". . . What?"

"PUT YOUR SHEETS IN HERE WHEN YOU'RE DONE."

"But . . . why?"

"Why not?"

"Look ma'am, I'm a cool guy. But I don't know what you're talking about. I'm confused and don't know what's going on. And it's not just because I'm off that gas nlah. Why are you telling me what dryer to use?" And it dawns on me, like the first ever sunrise on this sweet and sour earth, like an atomic shockwave sweeping through ancient ruins, like something doing something to something else, yet like nothing else. Reality. This woman. This fat woman with a bunch of makeup on. She's guarding and claiming the dryers she's sitting in front of as her own. Sentinel of the Loadstars. Three of them, none in use. That was why she told me of her plans, her intentions to use the three, which I didn't care about, because there's like three dozen dryers in here, and only two, three people. She could've used ten. She could've gotten in one and took a nap. I—and I couldn't seem to be able to stress this to her enough—didn't give a shit. She thought she was letting me use something that was never hers. Except she wasn't letting me. She was telling me. Benevolently commanding, now, that I do so. Myteetharefallingout.

"Oh, you said you wanted to use three. Right, yeah I was just gonna use this one over here."

"Yeah but I can use two. I'm just gonna spin them for a bit and hang them up at home. Use this one. It's bigger."

"I don't need to. It's just bedding."

"Just use it."

A standoff. Then this other, older woman chimes in. I didn't see her enter. It was like she was my guardian angel or something. Weathered skin with a dyke haircut. Badass bitch coming in hot. "You can use whatever dryer you want. This is a public place. You can't reserve machines [doing booze bottle motion with hand like 'that lady is drunk']."

"I guess I just don't understand what's it to you. Like what difference does it make, what dryer I use." And she didn't have an answer for that.

The lady that chimed in leaves and the fat woman starts going off on her. But I'm not paying attention. "What's up?"

"That woman. Saying all that. I know this is a public place. People need to get laundry done. Have some con-sideration."

I'm waiting for my bedding to finish washing. It stops, so I try to open the door. The fat woman corrects me. "You have to wait until the light turns off. The light's still on. It's still going."

"Ah." I wander over to the corkboard and take a picture of the meat cutter poster. I read a handwritten note from a guy trying to get a pool league together. It reminds me of my mom's masculine all-caps penwomanship. I hear the washer finish and the door click unlocked.

"There you go. **THERE** you **GOOOOO**."

I switch it over to the machine I fucking chose to use. I sit in a chair with my sunglasses on. My head is a stealth fighter jet. Worthless words deflecting off sharp angles, cruising undetected in enemy airspace. I text my friend Norm and tell him what's up.

"This is where you're a white belt in dealing with women. Sounds like you encountered a pretty typical older Michigan type lady, there may be some crossover. In general, they (when drunk or otherwise) must be harshly dealt with at first, and if they persist, which they usually don't, then completely ignore. They're basically doing an extreme version of female hitting on you. Negging if you will."

I pretend to fall asleep and can see the fat woman periodically glancing over the machines at me. I actually fall asleep, and when I wake, she's gone. I'm alone in the laundromat. The goal. My clothes are almost dry. I step outside for a stretch and some fresh air. I make eye contact with a dog in the passenger seat of a huge four-door pickup parked on the street out front. That badass older woman shuts the driver's side door and walks around the back of it.

"That's a beautiful, awesome-looking dog."

"Yeah, he's just a puppy still."

"Is he a Great Dane?"

"Yeah, he's a mix."

"Me too." We walk back inside together. "So I didn't know what was going on with that woman . . ."

"Summa these bitches who come in here are fucking nuts. Ya can't, like, call dibs on a machine you're not using."

"My grandma's friend warned me about this."

"When she started bossing you around, telling you to use that machine, that was when I decided to say something."

"Haha yeah, I think she saw you do that drinking gesture. That was hilarious."

"Oh yeah, she saw me. She was pissed. It seemed like she was drunk to me. When I first saw her, like from the side, I thought she had a black eye. Like her man gave her a shiner or something. Then I realized it was all that makeup."

"Duuude [burying face in hands while tearing up]."

"Haha right? I was trying to figure out what the deal was. If y'all were together or what. I was like 'I don't think this handsome guy is with this fuckin' . . . clown lookin' bitch.'"

"I don't know that person at all. Don't know her name. Never seen her before in my life. She just started talking at me. Minding my business for me."

"Yeah that's what I thought. And I didn't think she was your mom either."

"Oh FUCK no. That would be the apple falling on another planet from the tree."

"Right."

"My mom's gone. She was from here."

"I live a little ways up north. I work with horses."

"Damn. You and my mom would've gotten along I bet. Like as friends. You remind me of her friends. She was a really cool lady . . ."

"Aw man. That's sweet. My mom's been gone since August '94. [Long pause]. Have you ever seen The Drew Carey Show?"

"OH MY GOD THE WOMAN! WITH THE MAKE-UP! YESSS!!!"

We both cock our heads back and wail. We touch elbows with open smiles, sustaining an eye contact familiar for how new we are in each other's lives. We've always been right here, in this place together. I bag up my stuff and head out. I tell her I'll see her around, knowing it's true or at least wanting it to be.

But yesterday wasn't over yet. I went to a gem shop and bought moonstones. Incense. Rejuvenating balm. From a woman with blue hair. Our birthdays were two days apart. Geminis in the gem shop. I was doing better than I ever had before, but I still needed all the help I could get, and

I was trying new things, like not being so hard on myself, which my grandma said was probably why I was so unhappy all the time.

I got the fish fry back in town. A local known tweaker tried to talk to me at the bar. I let him talk, but I didn't let him in. Stealth fighter jet (nlah). He asked me if I was drinking Guinness. I said I wasn't and asked if he saw me drinking Guinness. He said yeah. I asked when. He said two years ago. I said I didn't really drink anymore. He said he wasn't trying to make me mad. I didn't say anything.

*

Today, which was yesterday. I start this story in the morning. I walk down the stairs in the early afternoon and the tweaker goes "Hey buddy, beautiful day."

"Sup man."

I get in my car and drive to the guy I'm seeing casually's house. It's a beautiful day. And guess what? He just got the new Zelda. He plays it while I work on this story and his roommate browses Grindr. We hear a bad car crash happen outside. Screams. I go upstairs to his bedroom, shut the windows and close the blinds, lay in his bed and continue working on this story. I hear sirens outside. I peek through the blinds and see a group of kids on the corner watching emergency personnel tend to the victims. I lay back down.

I go downstairs and ask casual guy if he wants to eat. We go to a grocery store and everything is seventy-five cents, so I buy everything. We make sandwiches back at his place and I ask to eat them inside even though it's a beautiful day. He tries the jalapeño chips I got. He says they're not too spicy, and he's thankful for me, because I get him to try new things, and trying new things is one of his core values. He asks me what my core values are. I say barbecue, sour cream and onion, sea salt and vinegar.

We go upstairs and have sex. I tell him I don't want to spend the night, because I have a family commitment in the morning. He says that's fine. I tell him I don't want to hurt him, and that if he says he wants more than what this is, I'm going to stop seeing him. I tell him my core values are honesty, loyalty, friendship, respect, and boundaries. We have popsicles downstairs and I leave.

Driving home at nightfall towards a crescent sliver moon

low above a hazy orange gloam, I pass at least a dozen cops. Getting into town, I pass an SUV with a missing front bumper, a decal across the top of its windshield that reads "BUT YOU DIDN'T DIE . . . YET."

*

Tomorrow, which was today. I slept in. I had coffee. I went and had brunch with my family. My cousin made Belgian waffles and a bunch of fixings from scratch. Strawberries, caramelized bananas, blueberry compote. Whipped cream. Scrambled farm fresh eggs that deep, rich color. It was bomb. I sat and ate and talked with my family in a circle. The world was on the verge of eating its own head. It seemed like everyone we knew was either dying of cancer or in the process of getting it. We had to admit, a lot of it was hilarious. Ridiculous. We gossiped and reminisced. I cracked some good jokes, and I laughed hard at what people said. I imagined my dead mom and boyfriend there with us. He told me he wanted to come here and meet my family and see this place and that never happened, but I know they would've loved him, because he loved me. I imagined my grandma imagining my grandpa and mom there. When my mom was dying, my grandma showed her old pictures from when she was growing up on the farm with all her siblings, to remember with her. My mom started crying. She said "we were all together then." A few months before she died, I told my mom my boyfriend had died. She started crying and said "I'm so sad for you" and held me. I wasn't sure if telling her would mean anything. I didn't want to just make her sad, only to watch her forget moments later what she was sad about. But I had to tell her. I had to let her be my mom.

Sometimes I can feel the presence of the dead so strong it's like they're breathing on me and touching me when I close my eyes. Like how a dream feels real when you're dreaming it and don't yet know it's a dream. You're just there, in that place, doing things. Just like I'm here, at my place, doing this. I'm talking to you. This is just from me to you. It's not for anybody else. It's not for them. It's for us. This is still our world. We've always been here. Forget the people with somehow both too much and not enough makeup. Standing behind you, claiming what's not theirs as theirs, looking over your shoulder, waiting for your light to go out. Forget the people trying to make their world your world, what they want, what you want. Forget them. The sirens outside. They're not about you. Let them miss you. Let these thoughts of yourself pass by. I have to go. The sun is coming up now. And it's going to shine. It's going to fucking shine whether you want it to or not. Nlah.

ABOUT THE AUTHOR:

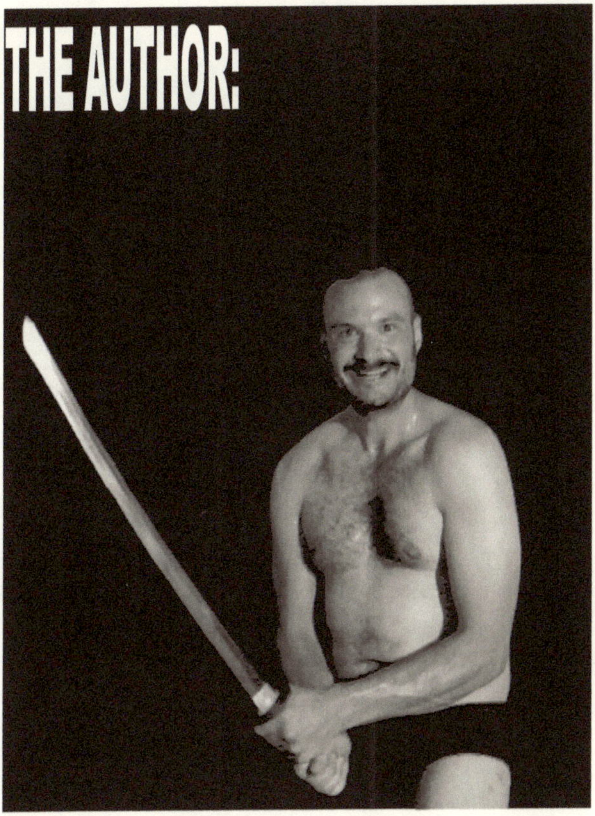

www.ingramcontent.com/pod-product-compliance
Lightning Source LLC
Chambersburg PA
CBHW020838020726
47497CB00005B/1156